Guns Across the Border

GUNS ACROSS
THE BORDER

John E. Lewis

AVALON BOOKS
THOMAS BOUREGY AND COMPANY, INC.
401 LAFAYETTE STREET
NEW YORK, NEW YORK 10002

PRINTED IN THE UNITED STATES OF AMERICA
BY HADDON CRAFTSMEN, SCRANTON, PENNSYLVANIA

Guns Across the Border

Chapter One

Beyond the mountains and the tops of the plateaus, the sky was a deep blue, a sudden glow spreading across the landscape as the sun slowly lifted. The valleys were still dark and quiet, and the only sound was the staccato pounding of the horses' hooves as the wagon rattled down the road.

Colonel Ford Taylor was tired, and there was a slight dull ache in his temples that bothered him constantly. Too many late nights, too much whiskey, and he could feel that he was getting older. At least he felt too old to be riding across these hills from southern Arizona into Mexico behind a team of horses.

He turned to King and smiled. "There's coffee in that pot under your part of the wagon seat. I don't know about you, but I could sure use some."

His companion had an American name, but it was obvious that he had some Mexican background. His dark

1

eyes looked out of a bronzed, healthy face, and it was topped by straight, jet-black hair. He wore a heavy sheepskin coat and a Stetson hat, and he shivered as he took the lid off the coffeepot and poured some of the dark liquid into the two tin cups.

"Is it always as cold as this?"

Taylor nodded as he took the cup from the other's hand. "It is at this time of the year. The wind comes right out of the mountains of northern Arizona, and the altitude is also a big factor. We're pretty high up here, even if it is in Mexico."

King peered off to the side of the wagon and looked into the rugged valley far below. "What would happen if the horses happened to slip over the edge?" he asked nervously.

Taylor laughed. "You're joking, of course."

King glanced back into the canyon and sighed. He had not been entirely joking with the question. "It becomes clearer all the time that you have been earning your money over the past few months."

Taylor slapped the reins across the backs of the horses and shrugged at the other man. "It doesn't worry me that much now. A couple more trips and I'm through. I've made this run too often. I'm living on borrowed time doing this. I'm going to request a transfer."

King frowned at that statement. "But, colonel," he protested. "There's no one else. What will we do?"

"There's always someone else," Taylor replied with a smile. "You can find him in some Army unit at Fort Bliss or Fort Huachuca. Plenty of former Civil War soldiers who will go anywhere and do anything if the assignment will further their career."

They moved on down the road, through landscape that was almost totally barren, without even cactus or sagebrush along the tops of the plateaus. Taylor handled the team of horses with the skill of an experienced expert. Finally they rode over the top of the ridge and down the other side.

Below them an enormous valley stretched for a great distance, dark with craggy rocks. Taylor reined the team up and sat and looked, and King sighed in the silence. "This is one of the most beautiful sights I have ever seen," he finally said.

Taylor smiled and urged the horses forward again, moving them into a gallop down the winding trail that led down the side of the mountain. King held his breath as the wagon came dangerously close to the edge of the road, and Taylor grinned over at him as the wagon careened along the trail.

"Now you know why the U.S. Army pays me as well as they do," Taylor yelled, to be heard above the noise of the wagon and the team.

King wiped his forehead, which was sweaty in spite of the coolness of the air. "I'm starting to get the idea," he shouted back. "How much farther?"

"Just a mile or so," the colonel told him. "Better be ready."

King reached behind the wagon seat and brought up a double-barreled Greenings shotgun and laid it across his lap. As they came around the bend, he could see a narrow river, tumbling through the rocks, widening almost into a shallow lake. Fifty yards off to the side, sheltered against the side of the hill, was an old Catholic mission, with a few small huts scattered in the area beyond it.

Taylor indicated the wide spot in front of the mission. "That's where we'll stop if we get the signal."

"And if we don't?"

"Then we'll turn right around and get out of here as quick as we can," Taylor said.

King looked at the blackened walls of the mission, where there had obviously been a fire, and at some of the holes in the wall. "What has happened here?" he asked.

"It was headquarters for the Mexican federal government forces a couple of years back when the local rebel army forces first invaded this area. There was a siege here for a couple of days, but it didn't last for long. The rebels brought in a couple of cannon and blew those holes in the walls."

"And then what?"

Taylor looked at him and shrugged. "They took everything that was worth anything, and then they killed all the defenders, including the Catholic monks who were there."

"Why? Was it just as a message to everyone else?"

Taylor nodded. "Basically," he responded. "Not that it has done them any good. In an area like this the rebel forces only control the small villages and towns, not all of the area in between."

On the other side of the ruined mission a torch suddenly flared up. Taylor pulled back on the reins and slowed the team and wagon in front of the old building.

"That's our signal," he said. "Everything is apparently all right."

The Mexican native women washing their clothing in the shallows a few yards away moved up onto the shore and watched the two men in the horse-drawn wagon. As they slowed up, a horseman, dressed in the uniform of the Mexican National Army, rode out from the other side of the mission.

"That's the man," Taylor said.

He looped the reins around the wooden seat and jumped down from the wagon. The uniformed lieutenant reined in his small mustang horse, dismounted, and strode toward them. He was fairly tall and muscular, with a deeply tanned and weathered face.

"His English isn't too good," Taylor said to King as the Mexican soldier approached them. "Speak Spanish to him and be sure to treat him with respect. He's a nobleman by birth, even though he's only a lieutenant. These people can be somewhat sensitive about things like that."

The Mexican grinned and held out his hand, and behind him several other men now rode up. "It is good to see you again, my friend," he said. "You have brought more guns for us?"

Taylor nodded as he shook hands. "Your men can unload them as soon as you like. I don't want to hang around here any longer than I have to."

The Mexican lieutenant shouted an order to his men, and he and Taylor and King moved to the side as the men started unloading the wagon.

"Pablo, this is Mr. King," Taylor said. "He is an officer in the American government. He is in charge of the people who have been supplying the guns and bullets I've been bringing you during the past six months."

Pablo shook King's hand warmly. "We Mexican men are fighters," he said proudly. "Your guns have helped us prove to the rebels that we can be better fighters than they are. Will you have some coffee and meat with us before you have to leave?"

King turned to Taylor. "Do we have time?" he asked.

Taylor shrugged. "We have that much time. It's okay with me."

Then Taylor offered the Mexican a cigarette. "Any rebels around here recently?" he asked casually.

"One group," Pablo answered. "Just six men. They were here about a week ago."

"What happened?"

The lieutenant grinned at him. "I'll show you after we have had our snack at the village."

They walked up the road toward the small houses, Pablo leading the horse that he had ridden in on.

"Mr. King has to make a special report to the American government in Washington about what is happening here," Taylor said. "He thought he would like to see things for himself."

"Just how strong are the rebels in this particular area?" King asked.

"Their nearest real strength is at a town called Joaquin, about fifty miles from here as the crow flies. Just a partial regiment there. No more than two hundred men. At some of the larger villages, like Juaramillo, which is thirty miles to the west, they keep a very large group of horsemen. In the military they are called cavalry. Basically, the hated rebel dogs just don't exist in the area between the villages."

They came to the outskirts of the village, a small place with huts built of sod and cedar brush. Several children ran along behind them, laughing and playing, but Taylor noticed that they kept a respectful distance from the lieutenant.

Then they came to a house near the center of the village, and Pablo opened the door and led the way in.

There were no windows in the confined space, and in the half dark Taylor was aware of the mud walls and the animal hides that were the covering for the floor. In a small pit in the center of the room, a small fire burned and an old Mexican woman was stirring the contents of a metal pot.

The three of them crouched down and waited. The old woman filled three metal cups from the pot and gave them one each. Then she passed them some dried beef jerky. Taylor drank his coffee down, and while he chewed on the beef, he passed his cup out for more.

"How are things going generally?" he asked.

Pablo shrugged noncommittally. "We will not be able to get the rebel leader or his forces here. We cannot hope to accomplish that much, because we are outnumbered. But we can keep them occupied and make their lives more miserable."

"What about guns?" King interjected. "Do you need more?"

"Of course. We can always use more," Pablo said.

"You were going to tell us about the rebel patrol that came in about a week ago," Taylor reminded him.

Pablo nodded and got to his feet. "If you have finished eating, I'll show you."

They moved back into the street and the lieutenant led the way back down the street to the mission. The doors hung askew, and the men walked through the open doorway between them.

As they walked into the courtyard, a flock of crows took off into the sunlight. Six mounds of freshly dug earth stood out starkly on the otherwise flat dirt of the mission courtyard.

"We were gone when they came," Pablo said simply. "When we got back, they were so busy terrorizing the women and children, they didn't even see us coming."

For a brief moment they looked at the six mounds which represented justice. Then the three of them turned, without speaking, and went back out through the mission doors into the roadway.

Pablo turned to Taylor. "What did you bring us this time?"

"A supply of the new repeating rifles and many hundred rounds of ammunition to go with them," Taylor answered.

Pablo nodded and smiled. "That's

good," he said, "but I could also use some dynamite next time you come."

Taylor looked at King with a question in his eyes. "Do you think you could manage that?" he asked.

King nodded thoughtfully. "I think so. Would two weeks from now be too soon for you?"

"Not for me," Taylor answered. "Just two more trips, and I'm going to request a transfer, anyway. The sooner I get those two trips in, the better I'll like it."

"Two weeks from now, then," Pablo said, and the three of them walked back to the wagon. The soldiers had finished unloading the wagon, and the boxes of rifles and ammunition were packed on burros and were headed out to where the *Federales* were camped in the nearby hills.

Taylor and King climbed up onto the wagon seat, and then King turned and reached down and shook hands with Pablo.

"Our government and yours are fighting together against the same enemy," King said.

Taylor slapped the reins across the backs of the two horses and turned the wagon in a large semicircle, to go back in the same direction from which they had come. Pablo waved to them, kicked his horse in the flanks, and galloped back toward the house of the village.

"Well," Taylor asked as they rode away, "what do you think?"

"I'm impressed," King said. "The whole thing is very interesting."

"I thought you would think so."

King lighted a cigarette, sat back against the board of the wagon seat, and sighed. "To you this is nothing, Ford. It's unpleasant and dangerous, but it's just another assignment in your Army career. It's something you do for money."

"And to you it's more like a holy crusade," Taylor said with a grin. "Personally, I had enough of the crusading thing in the War between the States."

"All right," King conceded, "enough of the philosophy. What about this dynamite that Lieutenant Pablo wants on the next trip? If I have it at the railhead at Nogales by next week, can you pick it up?"

"It's pushing it pretty close, but I can do it," Taylor said. "I'm bringing Major Lopez on a trip down here in the meantime. But if I move right along, I can be back to Nogales to pick up the explosives."

Another U.S. Army check deposited to his account in the Wells Fargo Bank, Taylor thought. He wasn't spending any money while he was making these trips. After two more trips he was through. He needed a transfer; he needed a rest from all of this.

After the two of them had ridden off, Pablo rode alongside the pack burros laden with the guns and ammunition. Then he rode into the village and dismounted.

Slowly the doors of the houses opened, and rebel soldiers who were not in uniform emerged. The door to Pablo's house opened and a young man, who was obviously a leader, came out. He wore two guns slung low on his legs and a full bullet belt crossed across his chest and hung over his shoulders. His hat was embroidered with an insignia of the rebellion.

"Did I do well?" Pablo asked him.

The young rebel officer smiled at him. "You did very well, my friend. Very well, indeed."

And the two stood and watched up the hillside where they could see the wagon, with Colonel Taylor and King, slowly disappearing in the distance.

Chapter Two

C olonel Ford Taylor stripped down his clothes and stepped into the big brass tub that had been filled with hot water by Raphael, the proprietor of the bathhouse. As Taylor sat and soaked, Raphael handed him a cup of strong, hot coffee, and he sipped it.

Jose Lopez stepped out from behind a curtain. He finished toweling himself down and started to get dressed. He was a Mexican of one of the ancient Aztec tribes, dark-skinned, mustached. A handsome man who stood six feet two, with a broad, muscular frame.

He smiled broadly at the man in the tub. "Feeling better, Ford? Headache gone?"

Taylor smiled back at him. "The headache seemed to slowly disappear as I rode out of Mexico. I'm ready for anything," he replied.

Raphael came back into the room with another bucket of hot water and poured

14

it into the tub. "Everything all right, Colonel Taylor?" he asked.

"You have made a new man out of me, Raphael," Taylor answered. "I could use you down in Sonora."

"Oh, no," the proprietor said in mock horror. "I'll stay in El Paso. Sonora is the edge of the earth."

He left the room then, and Ford Taylor lay back and looked up at the ceiling. "The edge of the earth—the dropping-off place." That certainly wasn't a bad description of Sonora. It was a barren and ugly land. Hopefully, Taylor thought, he would not have to face it many more times.

As he thought about that and sipped his coffee, Raphael stuck his head back into the room.

"Excuse me, Colonel Taylor, but there is a person out in the saloon waiting to see you."

The bathhouse was attached to the saloon and was reached by a connecting door.

"A person?" Taylor asked.

"A lady who says her name is Miss Carolyn Smith. An American lady," Raphael clarified.

"In this place?" Taylor asked.

Raphael merely shrugged. "This is

where you are," he said simply. Then he withdrew his head from the doorway.

Taylor stood up and stepped out of the tub. He took a towel and rubbed himself thoroughly. Then he pulled his pants on and slipped the shirt over his arms and shoulders.

He stepped through the connecting door into the cantina, followed by Raphael and Jose Lopez. They stood just inside the doorway and waited.

The woman standing rather self-consciously in the saloon was very attractive. She had long black hair and soft white skin. She was dressed in a simple cotton dress with a high neck.

She turned and faced Ford Taylor as he approached her. She saw a man in his late thirties. He was not tall, about five feet nine inches, but was very broad through the shoulders and chest. He had a capable look about him. He was not particularly handsome, but his face interested her. She could see that there was a seriousness, but she also detected a deep-seated humor there. He obviously did not take everything in life seriously.

She was as nervous as a schoolgirl as she stuck out her hand. "Colonel Taylor," she said, and the nervousness was obvious in her voice, "I'm Carolyn Smith."

He took her hand and flustered her even more by holding the hand longer than he needed to as dictated by etiquette. "You shouldn't be here, Miss Smith," he said, indicating the cantina around them. "It isn't anyplace for a lady."

"That's what the man at the hotel told me," she replied. "But I saw some other women here."

He merely smiled at that, and then she flushed as she realized her mistake.

He pulled out a chair from one of the tables and held it while she sat down. He sat across from her.

"What can I do for you?" Taylor asked.

"I'm trying to get to Sonora," she answered. "I was told that you can help me."

He frowned at her in obvious surprise. "I suppose that it's none of my business," he said, "but why on earth would you want to go to Sonora?"

"I'm a United States Army nurse," she explained. "I've been sent here by the government to escort Don Garcia's son from Mexico to the United States for treatment of his tuberculosis."

"So you're a nurse?"

"That's right," she answered.

"First visit to the West?" he asked.

She nodded. "My last Army tour included two years in the War between the States. Then I decided I would take some time off and visit California, so the government asked me to come by way of Texas and Mexico."

"That's certainly a detour," he said with a smile.

"Can you take me to Sonora?" she asked.

Taylor nodded. "There's no difficulty in that. There's plenty of room in the wagon. Just one other passenger will be with us—Major Jose Lopez of the Mexican Federal Army. We'll leave about four-thirty tomorrow morning. We'll make our first stop at Joaquin, and then in the next few days we'll ride on to Sonora. We'll get ready, and unless you have any problems in preparation, we'll leave at that time in the morning."

"I'm ready now," she assured him. "I'll be there first thing in the morning."

They got up from the table and walked together toward the saloon door. She said as they walked, "I forgot. I have a message for you from a Mr. Ferre."

He turned and looked at her. The expression in his eyes was now difficult for her to read. "Ferre? How did you meet Ferre?"

"On the train coming to El Paso. He was very kind to me. He said that he would like you to contact him at the usual place before you leave." She smiled cheerily. "It all sounds very mysterious."

He smiled somewhat cynically and ignored her unasked question. "Old Ferre always was one for a great joke," he said. "I won't be gone long."

Taylor went back to the bathhouse and picked up his leather jacket and gun belt and met her out in front of the saloon. Jose Lopez was standing beside her. Taylor was aware of a flash of irrational jealousy as he saw her standing with his handsome friend.

"I see that Jose has managed to make his own introductions, as usual," Taylor said.

"If I must be formally introduced, then I guess I must." Jose grinned devilishly at Carolyn, "Ford is a colonel in the United States Cavalry. He has never gotten over his original formal military training. They are very correct, you know."

He stood at attention, waiting for Taylor to present him—a handsome, challenging figure in his formal military dress.

Taylor looked at him and sighed in

mock distress. "I guess I'm trapped. Miss Carolyn Smith, may I present Major Jose Lopez, of the Mexican Federal Army. He is also a graduate of the United States Military Academy at West Point, I may add."

Jose took her hand and raised it to his lips. "I am charmed."

He gave his arm to Carolyn, and the three of them moved down the street to where they could look down on the wide Rio Grande River as it meandered through the center of the town.

Carolyn looked down at the muddy water. "It certainly looks dirty," she said.

"The natives here say that it's too thick to drink and too thin to plow," Taylor told her. "It does have a value, though. It irrigates a great deal of southern Texas and northern Mexico."

Down by the river there were several people involved in various activities. Some were fishing; some were cooking around small fires.

Carolyn looked at Jose. "May we walk down there and see the people?" she asked.

"Certainly. Anything you want."

"I'll leave you two," Taylor said. "If I'm going to go see Ferre before we leave, I'd better be moving. It's almost two o'clock now. I'll see you back at your hotel later."

He moved down the road quickly, and Carolyn watched him go, a slight frown on her face.

"Mr. Ferre told me that he was in the food business—a merchant," she said.

"That's right," Lopez said without expression. "Ford does some work with him. Ferre comes up to see him once a month. He has a small houseboat down on the Rio Grande here that he uses as an office."

"You said that Ford Taylor is a colonel in the cavalry?" she asked.

"Yes. He served under Ulysses S. Grant, and then he served in the Army of the Potomac," Lopez answered, but he said it in such an abrupt manner that Carolyn decided not to pursue the subject any more at that time.

Beyond the old part of town, down by the mud-and-adobe huts, a narrow path brought Taylor back down to the riverbank again. An old, small houseboat was tied up at the end of a small, rickety wharf.

Taylor walked out onto the wharf, his boots echoing on the planks, and then he stepped out onto the deck of the flat-bottomed boat. He looked inside the small cabin and saw Ferre sitting at a table. He went inside.

There were two glasses on the table filled with amber liquid, and Ferre offered Taylor one. He took it and sipped the drink.

"Hello, Ferre, you old son of a gun, you," Taylor said. "I got your message. It was delivered to me by a rather prim nurse lady in the saloon."

"She didn't!" Ferre said, almost shocked.

"I'm afraid she did," Taylor responded. "There's a lot about this area of Texas that Miss Smith doesn't know."

"I ran across her on the train down to El Paso," Ferre told him. "What's this about Don Garcia's son?"

"Apparently he has tuberculosis. There is certainly no place to treat it down there. Father Sacramente, the priest and doctor in Sonora, got word back. He asked them to send a doctor to escort the boy back here to the United States."

"So they sent an Army nurse," Ferre said.

"Sounds like the Army to me," Taylor said. "She was planning to travel across the country, so they took advantage of the situation."

"I wouldn't like to see her get hurt," Ferre said. "She seems like a nice woman."

"I said I'd take her down and bring her back, but it stops there. She's not under my command. She's not my responsibility," Taylor said shortly.

Ferre looked at him briefly and then changed the subject. "What information did you get for me this time? Did you do any mapping?"

Taylor took some folded pieces of paper from his pocket and pushed them across the table. "That's all of it. You now have the whole Mexican border from Fort Huachuca to Fort Bliss at El Paso."

"You've finished!"

Taylor nodded. "Time before last, I did my last mapmaking—did a good job too. King decided to ride with me this last time, so I didn't have complete and total freedom."

"The Department of State is still at it," Ferre mused. "I wonder what the Army would say if you told them about their competition in Washington."

"I don't care about all this political bickering," Taylor said. "Just two more trips and I'm finished with this whole

area. I'm requesting transfer. I already
told King that."

Ferre lit his pipe and stared thoughtfully at the man across the table. The in-
ternal affairs in Washington were about
as intriguing as the international affairs
between the United States and Mexico.

"How did you find things this trip?"
Ferre asked. "Any rebel-force activity?"

"There had been," Taylor said wryly.
"There were six new graves in the mission courtyard. Those represented the
way the federal soldiers had dealt with a
party of rebels."

"Nothing else? You're sure?" Ferre
persisted.

Taylor nodded at the question. "Pablo
says that all the activity has been either
down in the area of Mexico City or on the
east coast. There hasn't been a lot of apparent rebel interest in the border except
for a few isolated actions in the villages."

"That's pretty strange, you know,"
Ferre said, drawing on his pipe. "You
would think they'd be more concerned
with taking over the territory next to the
United States."

"I'm not sure if I care who owns the
territory," Taylor told him. "A month
from now I'll be transferred."

"Where are you going to be transferred?" Ferre asked as he sat back and looked at him.

"I don't really know, but I'm going to go somewhere. How long have I been working for you and the U.S. Secret Service, anyway?" Taylor went on. "I'm getting too old for this stuff. This is for younger men. I need a change."

"You've done us a good job," Ferre admitted. "But you've also been doing the Army a good job too. And you've been paid a colonel's pay for what you've done."

"All the money in the world won't help if I'm lying dead on the Mexican border," Taylor said laconically.

"Well, if you decide to get back in the business and help us some more and do more intelligence work for us, let me know," Ferre said pleasantly.

"You'll be the first to know," Taylor told him. "But don't depend on it."

He gulped down the last of the whiskey and set the glass down. Then he got up, turned, and walked out of the small cabin of the flat-bottom houseboat, stepped across to the landing, and walked back up the incline to the street.

Chapter Three

C arolyn finished sponging herself, using the porcelain basin in the bedroom of the hotel room. She dried herself and then pulled on her camisole and slip. She was pulling a gingham dress on over her head when there was a tapping on the door.

She called out quickly, "Who is it?"

"It's Jose Lopez."

She pulled the dress the rest of the way on and smoothed it down. Then she opened the door.

"Hello, Carolyn," he said. "I, uh, have made some arrangements for this evening. I'm rather pressed for time."

She smiled, suspecting that it must be a lady who was so important to him.

"Ford went to the stable to get the wagon ready for tomorrow," he went on. "He should be back shortly."

"Go ahead—I'll be all right," she said, and then with some devilment in her

26

eyes she added, "Better not keep her waiting."

He smiled at her. "Thanks for understanding," he said. "I'll see you tomorrow."

He left the doorway, and she shut the door and could hear the sound of his footsteps receding down the hallway.

She finished dressing and brushed her hair, watching herself in the mirror. When she was through, she put on a gray duster and walked down the hotel stairs to where the desk clerk was located.

"I'd like to go down to the main city stable," she told the clerk. "Is there any way I can get a buckboard or coach to take me?"

He looked at her a little strangely, almost as though she had perhaps taken leave of her senses. "Lady, this is El Paso," he finally said, as though that were explanation enough.

"Well, where is the stable?" she asked. "I'll walk."

That seemed to satisfy the clerk. "You go two blocks down the street this way," he said, pointing. "Then at the corner you go right for another block."

"Thank you," she said and left the hotel.

The wind was warm, as it usually was at this altitude in the desert. The sky was black but scattered with the pin-point torches of a million stars. The moon, about halfway through its phase, hung as if it had been cut from a piece of paper.

She walked past the people on the street, taking the directions given her by the hotel clerk.

The stable was set back off the street. There was one large building, and the wagon sat inside in the light of a single kerosene lantern, which was suspended from a beam across the ceiling.

Colonel Ford Taylor lounged against the wall of the building, watching as two men loaded boxes onto the wagon.

"What are these?" Taylor asked of a third man, who was obviously the leader of the group.

The man took out a Bowie knife and pried up the lid, showing wood shavings inside. He reached down inside of the shavings and pulled out a Winchester re-peating rifle, of the kind that was intro-duced in the last phases of the Civil War. The rifle was still greasy from the Cosmoline put on it at the armory where it had been made.

Taylor took the gun and looked at it. Engraved on the side in the metal were the words: *United States Army—Lees Ferry Arsenal.*

"Good grief!" he exclaimed. "Should we be going around advertising all over Mexico like this?"

"That's what the government sent, so that's what we deliver," the man answered somewhat defensively.

"I don't think that King is going to like that," Taylor said.

He put the rifle back in the box, and then he became aware that Carolyn Smith was standing just inside of the doorway.

"What are you doing here?" he demanded, his voice curt.

"I'm sorry," she said. "Jose Lopez has gone for the evening. Before he left he told me that you were here, so I came looking for you. I thought perhaps we could go to dinner or something."

He was somewhat mollified by her attitude and her explanation. "I think that's a very good idea," he said.

She looked at him for a minute, and then she looked at the boxes of rifles. "Jose said he thought you were loading food supplies and commodities," she said by way of further explanation.

Taylor turned to the three men. "You finish up here," he told them. He turned back to Carolyn. "How did you get here?" he asked.

"I walked from the hotel."

"Well, I guess we can also walk back to wherever we're going," he said.

He took hold of her arm and was aware of her coolness and restraint. He knew that she was upset by what she had seen and also that she was probably disappointed in him.

"I'm sorry if I spoiled any image you might have had of me," he said. "I am delivering guns to the Mexican army soldiers, who are trying to retain the order of things in Mexico. Major Jose Lopez is well aware of this," he added. "General Don Garcia also knows and approves of what I'm doing."

He took her hand as they walked down the street and would not let her pull away.

"It's coming to an end, anyway," he told her. "I'm applying for transfer. I would just as soon you knew about the whole thing."

"Go on," she said shortly.

"There's a Mexican-American named

King up at Sonora. He's supposed to be a merchant, but he's an agent of the U.S. State Department. He makes the arrangements for the guns and ammunition, and I run them over the border into Mexico, with the full approval of both the Mexican and American governments."

"To help the Mexican federal government fight against the rebellion?"

"Exactly."

She breathed an audible sigh of relief. "Oh, I'm so glad that's it."

He laughed in surprise. "That's an odd thing for a sweet, ladylike, American woman to say about war. And don't think that I'm a hero for it. I do it because it's my Army assignment," he went on.

"Do you think that the Mexican government can win, then?" she asked.

"I don't know. It's going to be difficult. Times are changing, and sometimes governments have a tendency to change with them." Then he abruptly changed the subject. "But where would you like to eat?"

"Oh, I think someplace that's local and colorful. Someplace that's a little bit out of the way. Not where the visitors to town eat, but where the local people eat."

"Sounds good," he said. "That way

you'll get an idea of some of the local customs and so on."

As they walked, he guided her away from the central part of El Paso, and they went to the old Mexican part of the town. He pushed open the doors to a small place that was marked by a little sign over the door proclaiming it to be Rosa's Cantina.

A small Mexican man, his eyes roving over Carolyn with open and frank admiration, approached them. He obviously knew Taylor, as he said, "A table, Senor Taylor? You wish to eat?"

"Yes, Manuel. We would like a table. Let's have one in the corner."

They threaded their way between the tables. The cantina was crowded, mostly with men. Carolyn was aware that many eyes followed her as the two of them walked to their table. She felt very uncomfortable.

They sat at the small table and Taylor ordered. It was a simple meal, but it was well cooked. It was highly spiced Mexican food, and Carolyn drank a lot of water to cool her burning mouth, but she enjoyed the meal nevertheless.

As they were finishing eating, the piano player and a drummer shattered the relative quiet with a fanfare. All eyes were centered in the middle of the floor, and a woman in a colorful full skirt and a flowered blouse began to dance around a large white sombrero in the middle of the floor. The dance got wilder and more exotic and more sensuous, and finally the dancer finished to wild applause and ran to the back of the cantina.

They were through eating, and Taylor thought that the mood of the crowd was such that it would be good for them to leave.

"Are you ready to go?" he asked.

"Yes," Carolyn said, her face somewhat pale. She had also sensed the change in the mood in the cantina.

They got up from the table and started out toward the door, Taylor's hand on her elbow guiding her. Suddenly one of the men at a close table reached out and grabbed at Carolyn. She turned and slapped him full in the face. The man's head snapped to the side, and the room became very still.

The man at the table started to his feet but was only partway up when Taylor hit him with a hard right fist in the jaw. The man's head jerked back, and he sprawled across the table. Taylor's right hand made a menacing move toward the six-gun on his hip, and no one else in the cantina moved.

He quickly grabbed Carolyn and guided her out the front door. No one moved to stop them. Outside on the street Taylor urged her on, turning and twisting through the alleyways of El Paso until they ended up on the main street overlooking the Rio Grande River.

"Why such a rush?" she asked him. "Do you think that they might follow us?"

"I'm sure they will. That young Mexican that you and I both hit back there in the cantina is the son of the mayor of El Paso."

"Will there be any trouble?" she asked.

"Nothing of the official kind, if that's what you mean. I'm sure that he'll send some of his hired hands after us, though," he told her.

"Did you have to treat him so roughly?" she asked. "I thought I had taken care of the situation."

He looked at her in some amusement, thinking that even though she was an Army nurse, there still were some aspects of the world she was a bit naive about.

"It doesn't pay to do things halfway," he said. "I thought I ought to get his attention. I'm sorry that I took you there in the first place."

"I'm not," she responded. "What happened wasn't your fault. I rather enjoyed being there and seeing some of the local color."

"Including some of the local lechers?" he asked with a grin.

"Well, I guess it gave me experience," she said with a laugh.

"You know, you hit hard for a nurse lady," he said.

"I do have a bit of a temper," she admitted.

He took her arm, and they walked along the road, watching the people still gathered along the edge of the river. Even though it was night, some were still fishing, and some were cooking over small fires.

"What do you do in northern Mexico besides deliver guns for the United States government and Mr. King?" she asked him.

"I do some mapmaking and surveying," he answered. "Sometimes I carry other cargo or passengers."

"I wouldn't have thought there was much demand for those kinds of things."

"Well, King has a pretty steady demand for the trips I make for him. Anyway, as I said, I'm going to be transferring soon. I'm tired of this kind of life, and I'm very tired of that place."

"What's it like?" she asked.

"Northern Mexico?" He shrugged. "A lot like New Mexico. It's barren, with treacherous mountains and plateaus. The main city of Bavispre includes a couple of thousand people, and it's much more like an overgrown village. When the winter comes, the elevation is high enough that it snows and it gets pretty uncomfortable. The roads, as we laughingly call them, are some of the worst in the whole North American continent."

"Tell me about Don Garcia."

"He's like a cougar, an old mountain lion. He's as proud as the devil himself. He has been quite a fighter in his day. He's something pretty special to his people too. You'll like his son, Xoactl. It's really a pity about his illness. I hope that you can get him to a sanitarium and get him cured."

"He's five, isn't he?"

"Yes. He'll turn six in three months."

"My instructions were to get in touch with a priest, a Father Sacramente, when I get there," she said.

"You'll like him. He's about sixty years old. A Catholic priest. He's been in this area of Mexico for years and doesn't have a single Catholic convert. But the people there love him"

"If he doesn't have any converts and doesn't have a congregation, what does he do about his priestly duties?" she asked.

"In addition to being a priest, he is also a qualified doctor. He runs a small mission hospital outside of Sonora. There's also one American up there, a man by the name of Winston Burt. He claims to be some kind of a surveyor or scientist or something."

"From the tone of your voice it doesn't sound like you like him very much," she said.

"Not much," he responded shortly. He stopped and scratched a Lucifer match to light a cigarette.

Then she asked, and her question was deliberately casual, "Why did the United States Army send you on a lonely, individual mission like this, Ford?"

"Do you really want to know?" he asked.

She didn't answer.

He finished lighting his cigarette and then said, "They sent me here as a disciplinary measure. It was either this or I would be retired—or rather, kicked out, which is the same for a career Army officer."

She could sense the pain in his voice. "What happened?" she asked softly.

"I was a cavalry officer during the War between the States. One morning we attacked a reinforced town. We did an excellent job with our attack. We killed twenty people—civilians—along with five of our own Union soldiers."

"But how could something like that happen?" she asked, the bewilderment showing in her voice.

"They gave me the wrong place on the map when they gave me the order to attack," he answered.

"Well, then, it wasn't your fault," she said.

"That depends on how you look at it. If I had checked the orders and the map more carefully, I would probably have spotted the error. But I was exhausted. There had been too much fighting, too many battles."

"But they didn't court-martial you?" she persisted.

"They didn't need to," he said with a wry smile. "Just a little chat with a man with a silver star on his shoulder and then the transfer to this assignment. I quickly got the message."

"I'm sorry, Ford," she said.

They had reached a point where a footpath led down from the road to the side of the river. As they paused for a moment, suddenly Carolyn screamed and Taylor ducked, turning to meet the rush from the darkness.

A fist grazed his jaw, and he lost his balance and fell, rolling over on the hard pan of the street. He sprang up and backed against the wall of a small house there by the side of the road. There were three men attacking him—dark, shadowy figures. Beyond them, farther down the street, stood the man Taylor and Carolyn had had trouble with in the cantina.

A knife gleamed in the light of the half moon, and Carolyn ran past the men to join Taylor against the wall.

"Kill him!" the man up the street yelled out. "Kill him!"

Taylor knew he was outnumbered, and he had no illusions about false heroics in the face of overwhelming odds. His hand dropped to the butt of his Colt .44 revolver and quickly drew it out. He fired one shot into the air, and the men in front of him stopped. There was no movement and there was silence.

"Go on! Get out of here!" Taylor yelled at them, and there was ice in his tone.

He quickly snapped off a shot in the general direction of the man down the street. The three close by him were already running away, and the mayor's son turned and disappeared into the night.

Taylor shoved the Colt back into its holster and said calmly to Carolyn, "I think that we'd better be going back to the hotel, don't you?"

She began to tremble, and he put his arm around her.

"It's all right," he told her. "Everything is all right now."

He bent his head down and kissed her gently on the lips, and she did not resist. Then, still keeping his arm around her, he started off toward the hotel.

Chapter Four

Ford Taylor gave the horses their head and let them go at their own rate of speed, merely using the reins to guide them along the winding road through the mountains.

Carolyn Smith sat beside him on the wooden seat, and Jose Lopez sat on a small jump seat behind her. She was wearing a warm sheepskin jacket that Taylor had provided her and some long riding pants that went all the way to her ankles.

Lopez poured coffee out of a metal pot into a tin cup and handed it to Carolyn.

They rode out of the shallow mountain pass and looked down into the valley below them. A broad river flowed through it between the sheer, jagged cliffs—a thread of silver in a landscape that was otherwise mostly gray and brown, dotted with occasional green sketches of sagebrush and scrub oak.

"To think that the new revolutionary

41

government of Mexico has laid claim to all of this wonderful land," Taylor said sarcastically.

"Why have they?" Carolyn asked.

"Well, it is part of Mexico," Jose said. "So if you're going to claim Mexico, you have to claim this part too. Also, it gives the people in the cities something to think about besides their poverty. You can claim a great military victory and give the people at home something to cheer about...in spite of their empty stomachs."

"I think you're both cynical," Carolyn said with a smile.

They came around a bend in the road and could see Sonora, its flat-roofed huts scattered across the broad plateau. General Don Garcia's hacienda stood off to the side, and Carolyn could identify it because of its larger size and its extensive yard and the stone fence that ran all the way around it.

They drove on down the road into the valley. As Taylor slowed the horses, another wagon came down the road to meet them. The two stopped, and Mr. King jumped down from the seat of the other wagon and came to meet them. The other man also got down from the buckboard. He was young and tanned and wore a six-gun on his right thigh, tied low in the manner of a professional gunslinger.

As he came forward, Jose Lopez looked at him, grinned wickedly, and said, "Why the six-gun, Winston? You usually don't carry one. Are you expecting trouble?"

The young man blushed at what he perceived to be criticism. "I'm going out doing some surveying for the next few days. Out here these days you just can't be too careful."

It was very obvious to Carolyn that there was a coolness between this young man and Taylor and Lopez.

"So this is Miss Smith?" King said, taking both of her hands in his. "We will do our best to make your stay here a pleasant one."

"You knew I was coming?" she asked.

Lopez grinned at the puzzlement in her voice. "I had the telegraph operator in El Paso send a message to alert Don Garcia."

King nodded. "Colonel Sandoval got the message," he said.

The young man turned from the back of the wagon. "You seem to be bringing in a lot of food supplies these days." Then he turned to Carolyn before Taylor could reply. "My name is Winston Burt, Miss Smith. I'm doing some geological mapping and survey work up here. If there is anything that I can do for you, please don't hesitate to ask."

"That's not very likely," Taylor said with acid in his voice.

Burt ignored him, holding Carolyn's hand longer than was necessary or even appropriate.

"That's very kind of you, Mr. Burt," she said.

"I'll be back in a couple of days," he told her. "It will probably take a few days for you to get the Garcia boy in condition to travel, so I hope you will still be here when I return."

He turned and walked back to his wagon, and King said, "I'll go ride back with Winston. Will you call on me this afternoon, Ford?"

"Yes. After we eat. I'll take Carolyn out to Father Sacramente's mission first. Is the boy still there?"

King nodded and smiled at Carolyn. "I'll have the pleasure of seeing you again, Miss Smith. Don Garcia is giving a small dinner party for you. He has invited me."

"I'll look forward to that, Mr. King."

The two men, Burt and King, rode off in their small buckboard. Watching them go, Carolyn pulled the sheepskin coat around her more tightly.

"It's cool up in these mountains," she said.

"We could be getting an early winter," Taylor replied. "I told you that it gets cold here. It's the altitude that causes it." Then he said to Jose Lopez, "I'll take Carolyn out to Father Sacramente now. What about you, Jose?"

Lopez looked back at him from gazing at the departing buckboard. "You can drop me at Colonel Sandoval's military headquarters. I'll no doubt see you both tonight at General Don Garcia's."

Taylor slapped the reins on the horses' backs and headed toward the town, following the rutted track that served as a road.

Carolyn looked around her as they rode into the town. The people were Mexican peasants, all dressed alike. Some stood and watched the wagon as it went by, stoic expressions on their faces.

"No one seems to be very happy," Carolyn said to no one in particular. "They're not smiling."

"This is a poor country and a hard land," Jose Lopez told her. "Life is hard, and they work from dawn until dark usually. It doesn't leave much time or incentive for laughter."

They pulled up in front of a barracks-like building with a man in uniform standing guard in front. Lopez jumped down from the wagon and took his canvas bag.

"I'll see you tonight," he told them.

Taylor and Carolyn rode on down the main street of the town and passed the hacienda of Don Garcia. Large cactus plants and yucca lined the pathway up to the house from the roadway. There was an elaborate plaster fountain in front, but no water came from it.

"Well, at least his place looks a little more inviting," Carolyn said.

Taylor smiled at her perception and her comment. "He's the general and the don," he said. "He has to keep up the appearances because of his position if nothing else."

They rode on out of town where the houses were more scattered. Then he pulled the wagon in through an arched entranceway and pulled up in front of a small adobe house.

"Is this one yours?" she asked, and he nodded.

He got down off the seat and a small,

graying woman, her face lined and wrinkled, opened the front door and came out onto the front porch, bowing at him in greeting.

"Your housekeeper?" Carolyn asked.

He nodded and reached for his carpetbag in the wagon. "I won't be but a minute," he said.

"Do you mind if I come in?" she asked. "I'd love to see inside."

He hesitated momentarily and then shrugged. "If you wish. But there really isn't much to see."

She followed him up the steps. On the porch he murmured something in Spanish to the old housekeeper, and she went inside. Then Taylor stood aside and said to Carolyn, "After you."

They were in the main living room. There was a stone fireplace, a brown bearskin rug on the floor, and the simplest of furniture. All in all, she thought, a typical bachelor's house.

"I'll be with you in a minute," Taylor said and crossed the room and went through another door.

She walked around the room, examining everything. There was a vase of curious workmanship on the small table, and she picked it up and looked at it. There was a slight sound from behind her, and she turned and saw a woman standing in the doorway to one of the rooms.

The woman was native, like the old housekeeper, but she was quite young. Her complexion was paler and flawless. She wore a purple velvet dress, like others of the native population that Carolyn had seen.

At the same moment, Ford Taylor came in from the bedroom. He said something quietly in Spanish, and the girl turned and disappeared through the doorway.

"Who was that?" Carolyn asked, not without a hint of jealousy in her voice.

"The housekeeper's daughter, Maria." He took the vase gently from her hands. "Do you like this?"

"Yes. Is it very old?" she asked almost automatically.

"This is probably Aztec. Tenth century or earlier. You'll find things like this all over the Bavispre area. The Aztecs were here back to antiquity. They were here when the Spanish came." He pulled out his pocket watch and looked at it. "We'd better get moving. It's almost eleven o'clock, and Father Sacramente holds his daily medical appointments at half-past

eleven. We ought to try to catch him before he starts with his patients."

They went out to the wagon, and he
helped her up onto the seat. They drove
away from his house as if nothing had
happened. But Carolyn did not feel the
same, and she did not feel like things
were the same. Therefore, there was a
constraint between them that had not
been there before.

Carolyn remembered the girl in his
house—her youth, the beauty of her
skin—and a jealous anger swept
through her. She knew that perhaps
there was nothing between the girl and
Taylor. Therefore, it wasn't reasonable of
her to feel this way, but the feeling was
there nevertheless.

The Catholic mission was on a slight
hill that rose above the river. It was a
flat-roofed, gray-stone building with a
carved wooden cross over the door. A few
sheep grazed right outside the mission,
and several people waited patiently.

Taylor slowed the wagon, and Carolyn
could see the evidence of disease that
was obvious on the people. Children were
suffering from ringworm and rickets, the
older people had obvious infections and

sores on their skin, and there was an occasional person with an arm in a sling.

"Surely Father Sacramente doesn't do this all on his own?" she asked Taylor incredulously.

"Don't ask me how he does it, but he does it," he answered. "He has a housekeeper to do his cooking and his cleaning. But he does all the doctoring."

Taylor carried Carolyn's cases up the steps, put them down, and spoke to the priest's housekeeper in Spanish. He came back down the steps and helped Carolyn down from the wagon.

"Father Sacramente is in the chapel," he told her.

They crossed the yard and went into the dim building. Up by the altar the candles flickered.

Father Sacramente came forward with a ready smile. "Ford, it is very good to see you again. And this must be Miss Smith. I heard from their telegraph that you were going to be here today."

"I feel like an imposter, Father," she said. "I believe that you were expecting a doctor, an actual physician."

"Nonsense. A qualified nurse with two years' experience in the United States Civil War will do for me any day of the week." He chuckled because she was obviously surprised that he knew so much about her. "Major Lopez is quite thorough in his telegraph messages," he went on in answer to her unasked question.

They walked to the main building. The medicine and equipment were arranged on shelves, and the stone walls and floor were quite well scrubbed, giving an overall impression of cleanliness and efficiency.

"This is where most of my work is done, and since I am the only doctor in hundreds of miles, the pace is usually fast and furious. You'll see for yourself how it goes in just a few minutes," Father Sacramente said.

"What about my patient?" Carolyn asked.

"Xoactl?" The priest sighed. "Frankly, he isn't doing well. He is staying here at the mission so I can watch him and better care for him. The general, Don Garcia, wanted me to stay at his hacienda, but, of course, I could not. I had to consider the welfare of my other patients, you know."

"So how is Xoactl getting along?" she persisted.

"He has been feverish, but we seem to be over the worst of that. Anyway, I

think he needs a few days of recupera-
tion before we take such a long journey."

"So Carolyn is going to stay here?"
Colonel Taylor asked.

"If she can stand a crotchety old man,"
Father Sacramente said, smiling. "Would
you like to see Xoactl?"

He led the way through a passageway
and opened a door. The boy looked very
pale and very frail as he slept, head
turned to one side on the pillow. They
withdrew and the priest shut the door.

Then he opened the door on the other
side of the hallway. It was a simple room
with a bed, a chair, and a closet.

"I'm afraid it is the best that I can do,"
he apologized.

"It's a palace compared to some of my
quarters during the war," Carolyn responded graciously.

They came back to the main room and
could see all the people waiting outside.

"I am late," the old priest said. "I'll
have to say good-bye for now, Ford. We'll
be seeing you this evening at Don Garcia's, won't we?"

"I imagine so," he answered.

"Could I be of help, Father?" Carolyn
asked.

The old man looked at her gratefully

and smiled. "I'd be glad to have your help. I'll find you a robe."

She nodded briefly at Taylor. "See you tonight, Ford."

She turned away and he could see an almost visible change. She was the professional now. She was a competent and assured nurse. She went with the priest to start seeing the first patients.

Taylor himself turned abruptly away. He pushed his way through the crowd, climbed up onto the seat of the wagon, slapped the reins across the horses' backs, and drove away.

Chapter Five

General Don Garcia sat at the head of the long table. The lamplight gleamed on the crystal and silverware on the table. He was now seventy years old, but he carried himself well. The face was that of a warrior, proud and strong, with the slight touch of arrogance of one who is born to rule.

There were six of them at the table besides the don: Carolyn, who had changed into her best dress for the formal occasion, and Ford Taylor on her left. Father Sacramente sat on the don's right, next to Mr. King, and Lopez and Colonel Diego Sandoval, commander of Don Garcia's small, personal military staff, faced each other.

"Father Sacramente has made you comfortable, Miss Smith?" Don Garcia asked.

"Yes," she said, smiling, "everything is fine."

"I would have liked to have you and

54

my son here at my hacienda," General Garcia said, "but this stubborn old priest here had to have his own way."

"And this stubborn old don would have had me forsake all my other patients," Father Sacramente countered in the bantering way of two men who were obviously good friends and who had known each other long enough that they could talk that way to each other.

"You have seen my son today?" Don Gardia asked Carolyn.

"Yes. He seems somewhat weak," she answered.

"I am very anxious that he start on his journey to your country," Don Garcia said. "I want him to be where he can be cured."

"I think he should wait a few more days until we can get him stronger," Father Sacramente said. "I think that Miss Smith agrees with me."

Carolyn nodded. "I believe that Father Sacramente is right."

Don Garcia lifted his hands in the air in a gesture of helplessness. "If you are in agreement with him, I bow before your decision. Shall we have brandy and cigars in the sitting room?"

King looked at Carolyn and smiled. "With Don Garcia's permission," he said, "perhaps I could show Miss Smith some of your treasures."

"Please do. You know my humble home. I would be very happy to have you guide our guest around."

They all stood, and King took Carolyn's arm and guided her out of the dining room. They walked down a hallway to a set of double doors.

"This is Don Garcia's library," King told her.

He opened the door and she waited just inside while he struck a Lucifer match and lighted three of the many coal-oil lanterns in the room.

Carolyn looked around her almost in awe. On the shelves was the most superb collection of pottery she had ever seen. There were the common earthen jars. Then there were alabaster vases—pale, translucent, and delicate looking. There were glazed urns in red and black, colors as vivid as the day they had been baked in the primitive ovens. From what Carolyn knew of the type, she could tell they were a collection of Aztec, Inca, and Mayan, some of them dating back into antiquity. There was also a collection of exquisite small idols.

She reached out and touched one of those figurines that was undoubtedly the figure of a god. It had obviously been discovered in pieces and put together painstakingly.

"Where was this discovered?" she asked.

"In a burial mound south of the city," King said. "There are a lot of places like that around here, showing the remains of some ancient civilizations."

Jose Lopez came into the room then, and Carolyn turned toward him. "Mr. King was showing me Don Garcia's collection of artifacts. I think it's very fascinating."

"Well, it's getting late," King said rather abruptly. "I really should be going. "I'll leave Miss Smith in your capable hands, major."

"He is an interesting person," she said after King had left the room.

"Do you like him?" Lopez asked.

"It's rather hard to say. He puts himself out to be pleasant, but I rather feel that there is a wall there. He seems to be wary, if you know what I mean."

"That's a good description. Would you like to see the general's gardens?"

"Why, yes, that would be nice," she answered.

They left the room and went out to the back of the hacienda. The moon shone through the dark branches of the cottonwood trees, and the night air was heavy with the scent of the blossoms of the various bushes and shrubs. There was a fountain made of light blue tile in the center of the garden. She sat down on the low wall that ringed the pool—a pool in which there was no water.

"This is beautiful," she said. "Like an oasis in the desert. But why is there no water in the fountains or the pool?"

"The time of year," he replied. "The dry summer season is just ending. Also, when winter comes here, it strikes suddenly. It can freeze overnight, and that would ruin the tile."

She gazed at the moon through the branches above. "Ford told me about the Civil War and what happened to him," she said.

Lopez looked down at her and smiled. "You like him, don't you?"

"Very much. He's quite different. Sometimes he seems bitter and can be violent. But sometimes he's very gentle."

"So here I am, trying to tell you how great another man is." Lopez sighed in mock sorrow. "What do you want to know about him?"

"Is there a woman in his life?" she asked. "Maria, for example."

"The housekeeper's daughter?" Lopez asked in surprise, and she nodded. "Now, Carolyn, that would not be right of me to tell, would it?" he chided gently and grinned.

She felt the anger of jealousy go through her. Even though Jose was joking, he did not answer her question directly.

"I think I'm in love with him," she said. "It's as simple as that."

"It's never as simple as that," Jose said, and he helped her to her feet. "I think we'd better go into the house."

"Is he as bitter about his war experience as he seems to be sometimes?" she persisted.

"Not really. It was an accident of war. Those things happen and he is intelligent enough to know that. But he loves the Army. Being sent here was a real loss to him."

"What does he believe in now?" she asked.

"More than he lets on. He pretends to be only interested in completing this tour of duty, but he betrays himself as a man of principles when a crisis comes."

"You like him a great deal, don't you?" she asked him.

"I value real friends and real friendship, Carolyn," he replied simply. "Colonel Ford Taylor has shown me that many times."

They walked back through the don's decorative gardens in silence. As they got to the steps of the house, Ford Taylor came out.

"There you are," he said. "Father Sacramente thinks that he should be going. I'll drive you both back in the buckboard."

"I'll get your coat," Lopez told Carolyn and went inside.

Taylor looked at Carolyn questioningly. "Did you have a nice time in the garden?" he asked, but there was more question than that in his voice. There was also a little hint of jealousy.

"Yes, thank you," she answered him lightly and brushed past him and went inside.

Taylor stood there in the semidarkness just outside the door, the aroma of her perfume lingering in his nostrils.

The three of them sat together on the buckboard seat on the way back to the mission, with Carolyn in the middle. Taylor was aware of her warmth and her softness pressed against him, and he experienced feelings that he had not experienced for some time.

When they got to the mission, Taylor helped the old priest down from the wagon seat and then assisted Carolyn as she got down from the buckboard. Father Sacramente bade them both good night and went inside.

Taylor stood close to her. Carolyn looked up at the half moon as clouds skidded across it and felt the warm wind on her face.

"It's a beautiful night," she said.

"It is," he agreed, "but there's a storm coming."

"How can you tell?"

"The direction of the wind and how warm it is," he answered. "I've been here before, remember."

Suddenly, as if to vindicate what he said, there was a flash of lightning and an almost immediate clap of thunder. Carolyn grasped out at him involuntarily, and he put his arms around her. As the next bolt of lightning flashed, he pulled her tight and kissed her full on the lips. She did not resist. Then, as they clung together, the first drops of rain spattered around them.

"I'd, uh, I'd better go in," she said breathlessly.

The door closed behind her, and Taylor swung up to the buckboard seat and started down the road as the rain pelted down.

He lay in bed that night and thought of Carolyn Smith and listened to the rain drumming on the roof. Finally he was able to drop off to sleep.

It was close to dawn when Taylor awakened, his sweat cold on his skin. He pulled the blanket up over his shoulders and started to go back to sleep. Then the sound that had awakened him came nearer and louder. It was the drumming of a horse's hooves. Then there was the sound of boots running across the courtyard. Taylor got quickly out of bed and pulled his pants on.

He moved to the door, and as he opened it and stepped outside, Winston Burt stumbled up the steps, his face wild in the early light of morning.

"For heaven's sake, Winston, what's wrong?" Taylor asked him.

"Rebel troops," Burt gasped. "At Hora. They overran my camp. Killed the workers."

"Rebels?" Taylor asked. "A patrol of them, you mean?"

"No. There were hundreds of them! Hundreds!" Burt panted.

Taylor stood still for just a few seconds, his mind working very rapidly. Then he pulled Burt inside the house and shut the door.

"Have you told anyone else about this?" Taylor asked.

Burt shook his head as he stood, gasping for breath, the water dripping from his coat.

"No. I haven't had time. I came here first," he answered.

"Good. If word gets out too soon, there will be a general panic, and we don't want that."

"No. No, we don't," Burt agreed, his voice trembling with fear.

"Now, this is what we're going to do," Taylor said. "We're going to the mission to warn Father Sacramente and Carolyn Smith. We'll leave them my buckboard, and they can follow us in with Xoactl as soon as they're ready."

"What do we do then?"

"We'll come back to town on horseback and break the news to General Garcia."

Taylor went back to the bedroom and dressed quickly, pulling on his boots and his shirt and jacket. He strapped his gun belt and holster on. Then he checked the cylinder of his Colt .44 and slid the six-gun into the holster.

As he started out the front door with Burt, the housekeeper's daughter, Maria, came into the living room.

"When will you be back?" she asked Taylor.

"I don't know," he told her. "But you and your mother will be all right here."

In just a few minutes she heard the sound of the horses' hooves.

Her mother came into the room. "You know what must be done," she said.

Marie pulled a jacket on and moved outside. She ran through the quiet streets in the early dawn, pelted by the rain. Within minutes she came to a small adobe house, ran up the steps, and knocked furiously on the wooden door.

"Mr. King! Mr. King!" she called loudly.

Chapter Six

It had been the rain that had saved Winston Burt—the sudden torrential downpour that turned a normally quiet mountain stream into the roaring torrent of a flash flood, in one place filling a dip in the road with its muddy cold water.

He had spent a long, hard day in the mountains by himself, exploring and making notes for his maps. Now, on his way back to his camp at Hora, the sudden rush of water confronted him as he rode down the trail.

Burt dismounted and tied his horse to a scrub oak. He found a branch and probed the depth of the water of the flash flood. It was at least four feet deep at that point. He didn't like to ride the horse across because he was afraid it might lose its footing and be swept away.

So he waded into the water. It was cold and it swirled around him, numbing him to the bone. He forced himself forward

65

and thrashed out with his arms. Then he finally got his feet onto solid ground and walked up out of the water.

He trudged along the muddy and rutted road, his head down against the driving rain. Somewhere up ahead he thought that he heard a cry and then another, confused shouting and the sharp, flat report of a gunshot, muffled by the rain. Seconds later came the *pow, pow, pow* of repeated firing.

Winston Burt stood at the top of a small rise, a slight frown on his face as he looked down through the trees at the flickering light of the campfire. There was a flurry of movement, the noise of men and horses and shouted commands.

Burt moved off the road and went down through the trees cautiously until he was no more than twenty yards from the camp, but above it on the hillside.

The valley was alive with rebel troops in various uniforms, guns in their hands, and Burt went cold inside. He could see two of his men standing beside the fire. Suddenly the soldiers opened fire and the two men crumpled, one of them toppling over into the burning embers.

The revolutionaries started going through the tents and the supplies that Burt had there. He decided he had seen enough. He turned and scrambled back up the hill, hoping that he had not been seen.

He put his head down and ran faster, one arm raised up in front of his face to ward off the tree branches. A moment later he floundered across the river again and staggered up the hill to where his horse was tethered.

Now, as he sat on his horse in the courtyard of the mission, remembering what had happened at Hora, Burt shivered involuntarily. He could hear the rise and fall of voices, and he looked at Father Sacramente and Colonel Ford Taylor standing in the doorway. After a minute, Father Sacramente went back inside, closing the door behind him, and Taylor ran down the steps and swung into the saddle of the second horse that Burt was holding.

"Okay, let's get moving," Taylor said.

"What did the priest have to say?" Burt asked as they urged their horses forward.

"What could he say? He's going to pack up as fast as he can and follow in the buckboard with Carolyn and the boy. There's no sense in his staying. You know what they do to people like him."

"What do you think the general, Don Garcia, will do?" Burt went on fearfully.

"What can he do except get out?" Taylor said. "If he crosses the border, he'll be safe. The rebels won't follow him. They won't dare incur the wrath of the United States Government."

"Why are they doing this?" Burt demanded as they rode side by side. "What could the revolutionaries want with a godforsaken place like this?"

"A paper victory," Taylor told him. "They will take some of the country they feel belongs to them and take the people's mind off the fact that the government controls Mexico City and the other population centers."

As the two rode down the deserted street, the sky was beginning to lighten over the mountains. Beyond the scattered flat-roofed houses, gray and somber, the river roared through the valley, swollen by the recent rain.

Later, at General Don Garcia's place, they waited in the same room where they had dined the night before. When the general came into the room, he was wearing his military uniform and standing ramrod straight.

"Now, Mr. Burt, perhaps you would be good enough to tell me in your own words what happened during the night at your camp," Don Garcia said.

When Burt had finished his story, Garcia turned to Taylor. "What do you think?"

"I don't understand," Taylor said. "I don't see why the rebels are invading and making a push here at this time."

"First I must talk to Colonel Diego Sandoval and Major Jose Lopez," Garcia said. "I have sent messengers telling them to meet me at the army head-quarters."

"You have seventy-five men," Taylor said. "They won't go far against a whole rebel army, and you can't rely on the local natives."

"That is a pessimistic view, but a correct one, I fear. You have a stagecoach at the stable in town. How many can you take out of here?" Garcia asked.

"Ten at the maximum, up over the mountains to the border. We stopped at the mission and left the buckboard. Father Sacramente is going to pack up as soon as he can and follow us with your son, Xoactl, and Miss Smith."

Don Garcia nodded as he digested the information. "Good," he said. "We must save my son at all costs."

"Then that gives us a possible list of

people to go out on the stagecoach. Yourself, Xoactl, Father Sacramente, Miss Smith, Burt, and Major Lopez. Colonel Sandoval, too, if he wants to go."

"What about King?" Burt interposed.

"I forgot about him," Taylor said, and then turned to Garcia. "Don Garcia is probably aware of what Mr. King has been doing here. No telling what the rebels will do if they get their hands on him."

The butler came back into the room and handed Don Garcia a leather belt and holster containing a Colt revolver. The general fastened it around his waist and smiled grimly. "Then I think it is time for us to move," he said. "You may drop me at Colonel Sandoval's headquarters. Then I suggest you continue on down to the stable and prepare the stagecoach so that we can leave immediately."

Outside it was completely light by now, the sky a uniform gray, the rain turning the dirt road into a quagmire as they rode down the street to the barracks building that was Colonel Diego Sandoval's headquarters.

As Don Garcia dismounted from the horse he was riding, Sandoval came out to meet him, with Lopez right behind him. Lopez looked up at Taylor, and Taylor shook his head grimly, as if he were answering a question. Then Taylor and Burt rode away quickly.

They galloped down the muddy road until they came to the dull, gray building that was the stable. They dismounted and Taylor pushed the door open wide, revealing the large stagecoach. A quiet, intense voice suddenly said, "All right, now move back away, please."

King came around the corner of the stable, a six-gun in one hand and a coal-oil lantern in another.

"Going somewhere, Ford?" he asked.

"That was the general idea," he answered suspiciously.

Ford Taylor moved his right hand casually so that his fingers were close to the butt of his Colt .44 revolver.

Marie, the housekeeper's daughter, moved from behind King and stood by his side.

"Well, I'll be . . ." Ford Taylor started.

King smiled, a tight-lipped smile without any humor behind it. "No one is going anywhere, Ford. It isn't part of the plan."

In a quick movement, King swung the coal-oil lantern in a wide arc and threw it into the stable so that it shattered against the side of the stagecoach and the flaming liquid spilled onto the straw of the stable.

At the same moment, Taylor pulled the Colt from its holster and fired a quick shot that went wild and splintered the door behind King's head, sending him running for cover.

Taylor turned and ran for his horse. Burt was already swinging back into his saddle. The stable quickly burst into one huge mass of flame as the two men dug their heels into their horses' flanks and galloped away.

King moved out from the side of the stable, holding his revolver with both hands and firing steadily, one shot after the other.

Burt and Taylor fired back at him as they rode into a ravine that started in the valley and slanted up the hillside, giving them some kind of cover from King's firing. They rode up out of the gully onto the side of the hill, where they could see below them.

King was standing a little aside from the burning stable, looking up toward them as they sat on their horses on the hillside. Marie lay sprawled awkwardly, like a rag doll, on the ground a short distance from King. Taylor didn't know what had happened to her, if King had shot her or if she had been hit by a stray bullet from him or Burt. It didn't really matter. Survival was the only thing that was important now.

The two men reined up on a ledge on the hillside, looking for the best way down. As the sat there on their horses, Burt yelled out and pointed.

Coming down the road toward the town, riding at a hard gallop, was a large group of the rebel soldiers. In the town there were cries of alarm. As the people scattered and started to run, the leading rebel soldiers aimed their rifles and fired, hitting buildings and people. All the revolutionaries were riding right through the town now, shooting as rapidly as they could at people, horses, and buildings.

"Let's get moving," Taylor shouted to Burt.

Winston Burt turned and looked at him, his face ashen and his eyes wide. "Down there? You must be crazy!"

Taylor didn't argue. He rode alongside Burt, leaned over and slapped Burt's horse on the rump. It began to gallop, and Taylor rode his own horse alongside. They went down the steep hillside and headed toward the town. The rebel horsemen had left, riding on down the road. Apparently, Taylor thought, it was intended only as a hit-and-run raid.

Fires had started in some of the buildings, and somewhere someone in the town was screaming monotonously.

Taylor and Burt reined up in front of Colonel Sandoval's headquarters. As Taylor dismounted, Jose Lopez staggered out of the building.

Taylor ran to him. "Are you all right?"

There was blood on Lopez's cheek, and he wiped it away. "I'm all right, just scratched," he said.

"What about Don Garcia?" Taylor asked.

"I don't know. He's inside someplace. They really shot the place up," Lopez said.

Burt got off his horse and joined them, and the three of them went inside the building.

Burt spoke, his voice trembling with fear, "We've got to get out of here, Ford! We just can't stay here!"

Taylor ignored him and turned to Lopez. "Where was General Garcia when the attack started?" he asked.

"In Colonel Sandoval's office. The room right in here."

There were two men lying on the floor

of the office. They were obviously dead.
Colonel Diego Sandoval knelt on the
floor beside the window, Don Garcia in
his arms.

Sandoval was covered with dust but
was apparently unhurt. Taylor crouched
down beside him and looked at Don Garcia. The nobleman's uniform had a large
spot of blood on the front, and death
stared from his eyes.

The don reached one hand feebly up
toward Taylor. "Xoactl," he rasped. "You
must save Xoactl. You promise?"

"Of course, general," Taylor told him.
"I will save him. You have my solemn
word on that."

Don Garcia choked. His hand grasped
futilely at the air, and he suddenly went
limp. Diego Sandoval gently laid him
down on his back on the floor.

Taylor stood up and turned to Lopez.
"Any sign of people from the mission?"
he asked.

Lopez shook his head, and then Burt
suddenly said, "I hope King rots in hell!"

Major Lopez looked at Taylor. He was
obviously puzzled. "What's he talking
about?"

"It seems that our good friend King
was working for the revolutionary army
all along. He just burned up the stable

and the stagecoach that we were going to leave in."

Lopez shook his head. "We thought we had checked him out," he said. "He was the liaison with the United States Government. He was providing the guns and ammunition for you to bring across the border to help us in our fight."

"Yes. And I guess he worked both sides of the fence all the time," Taylor said.

There was the sound of sudden sporadic gunfire, and they all turned and looked out the window. There was a small hill on the other side of the town. People were running toward the river, refugees from the town. There were men, women, and children, along with a few sheep and cattle.

Seconds later the top of the hill was alive with soldiers from the revolutionary army. They were the infantry soldiers who were following the initial sweep of the cavalry troops, those who had driven through the town and caused so much destruction. The infantry soldiers fired their rifles as they swept on, and the screams of the people rose in the air as many of them fell, wounded or dead.

Lopez turned to Sandoval. "We have about five minutes before they get here."

Winston Burt looked wildly around him and then suddenly rushed outside. When Taylor reached the door Burt was up on the seat of one of the wagons that had been standing outside. He was whipping the horses into motion, and as Taylor watched, the wagon disappeared down the road.

Lopez, standing behind Taylor, cursed savagely and then went back inside while Taylor stayed in the doorway. Suddenly a bullet splintered the doorway, and several rebel soldiers ran toward him down the road. He ducked back inside as Lopez appeared at a window and fired a repeating rifle rapidly at the rabble of soldiers, driving them back.

Colonel Sandoval shouted, "From the looks of things, we had better get moving! Every man for himself and the devil take the hindmost. Try to get across the river. There's a village called Donado ten miles to the north. We'll meet there."

The rear door of the headquarters led into a fenced yard. One of Sandoval's men climbed up onto the fence and swung his leg over. There was a sudden yell, and a group of the rebels appeared about thirty yards to the left. Several of them fired at once, and the man on the fence screamed and fell backward into the yard, clutching his chest.

Sandoval scrambled through a hole in the fence and started up the slope, and Taylor went after him. They dodged and weaved frantically from side to side as the rebel army soldiers continued to fire at them. Taylor was aware that Lopez was hard on his heels, and then he saw Sandoval disappearing over the top of the hill.

Taylor clawed his way up, slipping and sliding on the wet ground. He went up over the top of the hill with his head down, gasping for breath, and then he tripped and fell.

He had a brief impression of Sandoval sliding down the steep slope of shale to the river below, and then he saw him plunge into the water. Lopez was lying on the ground a few yards away. A soldier stood over him with his rifle aimed down, pointed directly at him.

Taylor got to his feet and backed up against a rock, and the rebel soldiers closed in on him.

Chapter Seven

The building housing the town jail had been left intact by the rebels, and, from the small cell, Ford Taylor had an interesting view of the town from the window.

It was ten o'clock in the morning. Four hours had passed since the initial attack from the rebel army. The weather was chilly, and the rain drifted through the bars into Taylor's face. He looked back into the room.

"I'll bet it's going to be an early winter," he commented.

"For you and me that hardly matters. Our future is of little importance," Lopez said.

"You think so?" Taylor asked.

There was the sound of sustained rifle fire from the direction of the river, and Lopez smiled wanly. "There's your answer," he said. "Those firing squads haven't stopped since early morning."

"Then why have they let us last this

79

long? Why are they giving us special treatment?" Taylor asked.

There was no time for Lopez to answer. A key turned in the lock of the cell door. The door swung open and a soldier stepped in. Another soldier stood at the door with his rifle leveled. Lopez got up and the first man said, "Not you, him," pointing to Taylor.

Three rebel soldiers took Taylor out of the cell, and they locked the door again. One soldier walked down the corridor with Taylor following him, and the two other soldiers came along behind, with their rifles at the ready. They came to a door where the first rebel knocked and then led the way in.

A rebel army officer stood there, staring at the fire in the small fireplace. He wore a heavy military overcoat which carried epaulets showing the insignia of a full colonel. He turned and looked at Taylor calmly without smiling.

"You don't look too good, Ford."

"I think you're responsible for that, King," Taylor responded.

"It's nothing personal, Ford. We just happened to be on different sides of this war."

"So you're a spy?" Taylor asked.

"That's one term for it. I suppose you could call it that."

"How long have you been making fools out of the people in Washington?" Taylor asked him.

King smiled now for the first time since Taylor had entered the room.

"I have never been to Washington. The United States Government did have an agent named King and they did send him out west to Texas. He got as far as El Paso, and I took his place."

"What about the guns I brought across the border? What about Pablo and his men?" Taylor asked. "Was all that a fake too?"

"The guns have been very useful to us," King replied. "It also worked as an elaborate ruse to allow me to move freely back and forth across the border, to keep in touch and keep an eye on the federal army leaders like Don Garcia, and to prepare the way for the revolutionary government of Mexico to take over the land that legally belongs to them and to the people."

"I don't need the political speeches," Taylor said caustically. "Where did Maria fit in?"

"She and her mother were of no real importance. I paid them to keep me informed of your movements. They did that job adequately for me."

"You speak in the past tense."

"Only as far as Maria is concerned. She was killed back at the stable," King said without emotion.

Thinking about how his housekeeper and her daughter had betrayed him, Ford Taylor decided he really had no regrets.

"Do you think you can get away with this?" he asked, realizing how trite his question sounded.

"Why not?" King said blandly. "The United States will not interfere. All they want right now is to officially maintain the status quo and to keep the border quiet. They are not going to come over into Mexico and dabble in our affairs."

"You've got it all worked out, haven't you?"

"I think so. Except for one important detail. Don Garcia is now dead, which is helpful. But these native people are rather superstitious and tied to the past. They revered General Don Garcia as a great leader. His son, Xoactl, is his successor as the don."

"So he is an obstacle to your taking over?" Taylor asked.

"Not at all," King said, smiling. "With

our help and guidance he could be very helpful to us in showing his people the correct way to go."

"I see," Taylor responded dryly.

"Good. Then perhaps you will help me in this matter. Things could go easier for you. Where is the boy now?" King asked.

Taylor looked at him in honest astonishment. "You mean you don't know?"

"He is not at the Catholic mission," King replied. "Neither is Father Sacramente nor the American nurse. We have spent some time searching the mission and the town."

Taylor felt a flood of relief through him at the news that perhaps they had escaped. "And you want me to help?" he asked, somewhat incredulously.

"I know that you went straight to the mission when you left your house after Winston Burt came and told you about the invasion. Maria told me."

Taylor felt that he might as well tell the man the truth. There was no point in lying. "That's right," he said. "We left my buckboard and told Father Sacramente to pack up as soon as he could and meet us at the stable and the stagecoach. I guess your men moved too fast for him."

"But I haven't been able to find Winston Burt, either," King said. "You must have arranged an alternate plan in case you needed it."

Taylor shrugged.

"You might find it wise to cooperate," King said. "I can make things very difficult for you."

"I've told you all I know," Taylor said. "What more can I do? You're wasting your time."

Colonel King stared at him. There was no expression on his face. "All right, sergeant," he finally said to the soldier. "Take him away and bring Major Lopez in to me."

Taylor turned to go. "Now you *are* wasting your time," he said with a wry smile as he went out.

The revolutionary army headquarters had been set up at Don Garcia's hacienda, and the commanding officer, General Rolando Vigil, stood on the terrace and looked out over the garden.

He was obviously not happy and tapped his fingers impatiently on the railing. He heard a noise and turned to find King in the room behind him.

"You have found him?" he demanded.

"Not yet, general."

"This is your responsibility, colonel,"

the general said angrily. "I expected the boy to be here waiting when I got here."

"Apparently the priest and the American nurse left the mission with the boy shortly before our men got here," King explained. "I have just received a report that their buckboard was found ten miles north of here. There was a ferry boat there, so I assume that they have crossed the river. A wagon driven by the man called Burt was found by the patrol in the same place."

"Has the patrol gone after them?" the general persisted.

"There were no other boats, so they could not," King said. "And the river is swollen with the rains."

"Is there anyplace where the river can be crossed?" the general demanded.

"Certainly not here, sir. The current is even too swift for a ferry boat."

King spread out a rough map on the hardwood dining table and pointed. "Fifteen miles north of here the river is wide and shallow. There is only the one road to the United States from here—that is the shortest distance—and they are now on foot. They must stay on the road. The priest is old, and they also have a small boy. We should be able to catch them easily."

General Vigil nodded grimly. "Let us hope so, for your sake, colonel. I will send other patrols down this side of the river. They should find boats sooner or later. Once across the river, they can proceed on foot and head these people off on the road ahead of you."

"A very good idea, sir."

The general studied the map for a brief time. Then he looked up. "This Colonel Taylor that you spoke of. You are certain that he knows nothing?"

"It is difficult to be sure," King answered. "And Major Lopez is also very stubborn."

"Have you exhausted the usual methods of questioning?" the general asked.

"They take time, general, and are sometimes fatal. Colonel Taylor should be preserved for a more thorough questioning."

"Why is that?"

"We know that he has been working as an intelligence officer for the United States Government," King said.

"I see!" the general responded emphatically.

King looked at the general for a moment and hesitated. Then he said, "I would like to try one more time before my men and I leave, just in case those two do have some information of value. There is a plan we have used before which often has results."

"It sounds interesting," General Vigil said. "I think I will go with you. I sincerely hope that we are not wasting our time on this plan that you have in mind."

The wind was bitter and cold, and Taylor shivered as it seemed to go clear through him as they sat out in the field. Lopez was next to him. In a line beyond were several of Colonel Diego Sandoval's men, all of them kneeling side by side in the mud.

Two covered wagons sat nearby. Many of the rebel soldiers were sitting in them, trying to keep out of the cold and the rain. A few stood guard out in the open, covering the kneeling men with their rifles.

Two men rode up on horseback, and Lopez turned toward Taylor and said, "We have company, Ford."

Colonel King walked across the ground toward them, with General Vigil at his side. The two of them paused a few yards away, and the general asked, "These are the two men?"

King nodded and said, "They both speak Spanish."

"Excellent." The general walked closer to them. "Let us not waste any more time. We want to know the whereabouts of the Catholic priest and the young don. If you are sensible and help us, you will be treated better than if you resist."

Taylor and Lopez stared up at him from where they were kneeling in the mud, but neither of them responded. They merely looked at him without expression.

King sighed with obvious exasperation. "You are a fool, Ford," he said. "We've found the buckboard, so we know that they've crossed the river. They won't get far whether you help us or not."

King and the general turned and walked back to the covered wagons. The general climbed inside one of them with his troops to get out of the rain.

King spoke to the rebel sergeant who was in charge. "Go ahead. You have your orders. Execute them all, starting at the beginning of the line. But stop firing before you reach the American and the Mexican major. I don't want you harming either one of them."

He climbed into the back of the covered wagon beside the general, who smiled at him. "This should prove to be most interesting, colonel," he said.

Taylor stared at the ground, waiting for what obviously was to come. He wondered about Father Sacramente and Carolyn and Xoactl, and he prayed that the priest would have sense enough to keep on moving. But the Unites States border was still a long way off.

The rebel soliders came toward them. One of the soldiers kicked him and then handed him a shovel. They were apparently to dig their own graves. Ford struggled to his feet with difficulty. The dirt was soft, and he knew that the digging of the necessary hole would not take long.

The rain increased into a downpour, and the soldiers turned and ran to the shelter of the covered wagons, leaving one man standing guard, his rifle crooked in his arm.

Taylor stopped shoveling for a minute to rest, and Lopez moved closer to him.

"I don't suppose we've got much longer," Taylor said.

"Not if I can help it," Lopez muttered under his breath. Then he asked, "How good are you at running, Ford?"

"Fair. But what are you talking about?" he asked, confused.

"This," Lopez said and slapped him across the face.

Taylor staggered back, and the guard immediately hurried over to see what the fighting was about. He leaned down toward them as they stood in the hole they had dug, the repeating rifle pointed threateningly. Suddenly Lopez swung the shovel around and hit the soldier in the back of the head with it. The man fell into the hole they had dug and made no sound.

Lopez grabbed the guard's rifle and ran toward the river. Taylor followed right behind him, slipping and stumbling in the mud. Taylor looked over his shoulder and saw the other prisoners, scattered all across the field and running for their lives. The first rebel army soldiers had jumped out of the wagons and had begun firing at the escaping prisoners.

Together Lopez and Taylor reached the river. The river was muddy and very swift. Logs and branches floated by at a fast rate that indicated how difficult it would be to reach the other side.

One of Colonel Sandoval's men, a corporal, ran past them and threw himself into the river. The current swiftly carried him out of sight. Others followed, some bleeding from wounds, but they all dived into the raging river as the only hope that they had of ultimately escaping.

A bullet hit the ground at Taylor's feet, kicking up the dirt. Lopez turned and saw four of the soldiers at the top of the hill. He fired the repeating rifle rapidly, and two of the soldiers fell to the ground. The other two disappeared behind the hill as Lopez levered the bullets quickly into the rifle and rapidly emptied the gun in the direction of the rebels.

Then Lopez threw the gun away from him since it was empty, and he and Taylor ran into the water and made their way into the brush and tamarack that grew along the shore. The water felt bitter cold, and they began to move farther downstream in order to get out of sight of the soldiers.

They pushed through the tamarack, and there was a floating mass of trees and branches. They moved out into the branches so they could not be seen from the shore. Then the two of them rested side by side, holding on to some branches and gasping for breath. From the shore they could hear the voices of the rebel army soldiers as the revolutionaries searched for them.

"Now what?" Taylor asked.

"We'll have to try to get across the river on one of these logs," Lopez said. "They will be all over this side of the bank. We can't get out here."

He let go of the branches and splashed his way to the next tree, moving slowly through the floating branches, and Taylor followed him. When they reached the outside edge of the mass, they found a large tree that was just barely hanging to some of the limbs projecting out into the river.

Lopez pulled himself to the front end of the tree, and Taylor said, "I'll try to guide it from the back end."

Together they pushed and got the tree out into the current. In a few minutes they were drifting rapidly away from the shore and down the river. Taylor found that there was no way he could guide the tree. It went with the current. All he could do was to hang on and float through the chilly water.

When Colonel King came back up from the riverbank he found General Vigil still sitting under the canvas cover of the wagon.

"Well?" the general said icily.

"There is no sign of them, general," King reported.

"Your small plan which may lead to remarkable results. Right?" the general said sarcastically.

He was not smiling. King watched him, shrugged and said, "I'm sorry, sir. What else can I say?"

"Nothing!" the general told him sharply. "It would be best if you said nothing. With the river like it is, it is very likely that Taylor and Lopez have already drowned. Let us hope for your sake that is the case. Anyway, colonel, take your men north to where you can cross the river. Bring me back Xoactl Garcia. Without him, you might as well not come back at all. Do you understand me?"

King's face was almost white as he faced the general. Then, without comment, he saluted and turned away.

Chapter Eight

J ose Lopez was still at the front end of the tree as they floated downstream. "I can see that we're getting close to the other side," he said softly to Taylor.

Suddenly the bank was very close, and then, with a bump, the tree hit the edge. Taylor and Lopez found that they could stand on the bottom and be only waist deep in the water. Slowly they struggled their way out of the river and up onto the bank.

The two men stood and looked across the river, listening, but there was no sign of their pursuers. They were both shaking with the wet and the cold.

"Sooner or later they'll get men across by boat," Lopez said.

"But they'll still be on foot, just like we are," Taylor told him. "They've got to go a lot farther north to get their horses and wagons across."

"Well, one thing is certain," Lopez said with a wry grin. "There's only one logical main road out of here to the United States, and there's only one way that we're going to get to it."

They turned from the river and started walking through the rain. Lopez was in the lead, and when he got to the top of a small rise, he stopped quickly. Taylor caught up with him. Down in the area below them was a small adobe hut all by itself.

There was no sign of life around it, and they moved cautiously. When they got to the small building, Lopez eased the door open and led the way in.

The place was dirty and it smelled, but it was warmer than the outside, and at least it was dry. For the moment those things mattered more than anything else. Taylor put some wood in the small stone fireplace in the corner and finally got the fire to light.

Lopez was rummaging around in a small cupboard in the opposite corner. Finally he gave a shout of triumph.

"Some beef jerky and some moldy cheese!" he said. "It may not be the best, but it's sure better than nothing."

They built the fire up and sat in front of it and ate the food.

"You know," Taylor said, "it's certainly too bad Mother isn't here."

Lopez looked at him, thoroughly puzzled. "Why is that?" he asked.

"Well, she never has any fun," Taylor said, and they both laughed heartily.

It felt good to be able to laugh together and let some of their emotions out after the tension and the physical exertions of the past several hours. After they had finished eating, they lay down on the dirt floor in front of the fire and slept.

Taylor woke up slowly, having a little trouble remembering where he was. Finally he sat up. Lopez was squatting by the fire.

"How do you feel?" he asked him.

"Just terrible, thank you," Taylor answered. "How long have we been here?"

"Just a couple of hours," Lopez answered. "We'd better get moving. At least our clothes are drier than they were, and we've had something to eat." He peered out through the small window and then went on, "From the looks of it, the rain isn't going to let up. It will probably change to snow."

"That's all we need," Taylor said.

Lopez turned from the window and shrugged. "That isn't all bad. It will make things just as bad for the rebels. However," he went on, "it means that we will have to move fast. We must be about six or seven miles from the road here. Anyone else who got across the river has to move in the same direction. They really have no other choice."

"You mean Carolyn and Father Sacramente?"

"Or Diego Sandoval. But the revolutionary soldiers will follow the same route once they get across, and we have to keep ahead of them. If we can reach the village Colonel Sandoval mentioned —Donado—and get some horses, then we might stand a chance."

Lopez picked up a couple of worn and dirty serapes from the corner of the hut and tossed one over to Taylor.

"We might wear these over our shoulders. It will keep out some of the rain and the cold."

Taylor looked at the serape somewhat distastefully. "I guess it would do that, all right," he said without enthusiasm.

Suddenly Lopez drew back from the doorway and put a finger to his lips. Then Taylor heard it, too, the sound of footsteps on the wet ground outside. As the sound of steps approached the hut, Lopez threw himself through the doorway. There was the sound of a struggle outside.

Taylor went out the doorway, fists ready, but he could see that there was no need for him to involve himself physically. Lopez stood over a man crouched on the ground in the mud. The tattered remnants of a uniform with corporal's stripes still clung to the man's body.

"That's the man who went into the river ahead of us," Taylor said. "He's one of Colonel Sandoval's men."

"You remember me, Major Lopez," the man said, grinning from his position on the ground. "I am Corporal Martinez."

Lopez laughed, as much in relief as anything.

"I know you, all right," he said and helped the man to his feet.

The three of them went inside, and Martinez warmed himself in front of the fire.

"What are we going to do?" Taylor asked. "We can't take a couple of hours more for Martinez to dry himself off."

"There is no need, sir," Martinez said. He picked up one of the serapes from the corner of the small room. "I'll just throw this over me."

"There's some of that moldy cheese left," Lopez told him. "You can take it with you and eat it while we go."

"Where are we headed, sir?" Martinez asked.

"To the road out of this cursed place. Colonel Sandoval told us to meet at Donado if we got across the river. Do you know where that place is?"

"It's about eight miles to the north," Martinez said. "I can guide you there."

The three of them left the cabin and moved on. The rain kept coming steadily. They had been going for about half an hour when Lopez stopped them.

"Listen," he said. "I thought I heard firing."

They stood and listened, and then it sounded again, a faint echo in the rain.

"It sounds like rifle fire," Taylor said.

"Probably back across the river," Lopez said. "We're still parallel with it. But maybe one of us should scout ahead."

"I'll go, sir," Martinez said and quickly moved out in front.

They had been walking for about another half mile when suddenly Martinez came back.

"What is it?" Lopez asked.

"There is a village up ahead, sir," Martinez said.

"Good. Lead the way."

They went over a nearby hill, and the

small village was ahead of them. There were only six houses clustered together. There was the smell of wood smoke in the air.

The three men came to the first house, and Martinez opened the door and went in. He came out a moment later.

"Empty, sir. Everything is gone. There is no one or nothing."

They went from hut to hut with the same results. Everyone and everything was gone. In the last house the embers of a fire still glowed in the fireplace.

"They must have heard about the invasion," Lopez said. "They've gone and taken their horses, cattle, sheep, and the lot. I suppose they've gone to the hills to wait things out."

Martinez looked at the two of them questioningly. "We move on now, sirs? No reason to stay here?"

"That's right, Martinez," Taylor said. "There's no reason for us to stay here."

They moved away from the small cluster of houses. The ground began to slope more steeply, and the air seemed to be a little colder.

"We must be coming to the edge of the valley," Lopez said. "And that means the road can't be far away. We should reach it in another mile or so."

They slowly made their way down the hillside. Finally they were on the lower foothills and the going was easier.

Martinez had been scouting ahead again, and now he came back. "Donado is just below in the valley, sir," he said to Lopez. "There are four wagons stopped there."

They covered the rest of the distance quickly, running down the slopes until they scrambled up onto the roadbed. They moved down the road toward the wagons. Father Sacramente was standing talking to a tall, muscular man dressed in a sheepskin jacket.

Taylor's feet scuffed on the ground, and the two men turned around. The tall man in the sheepskin jacket was Colonel Diego Sandoval.

"Praise God," the priest said when he saw Taylor and Lopez.

The canvas flap on one of the wagons was pushed aside, and Carolyn Smith climbed out of the back of the wagon. She ran toward Ford Taylor, and the joy in her eyes and on her face was obvious.

Chapter Nine

A corporal and three privates came forward and behind them, his left arm heavily bandaged, came Winston Burt.

"We didn't expect to see any of you alive again," Father Sacramente said. "The rebel soldiers arrived so quickly that we barely got out of the mission. I drove the buckboard up the river to the ferry, but it had been destroyed. Everyone in the village was being taken across the river in small boats."

"Mr. Burt came while we were waiting for a boat," Carolyn said. "He had been badly wounded. He told us what happened at Sonora. He thought that he was the only one to get away."

"He was for a while," Lopez said dryly and looked pointedly at Burt.

Burt looked very pale and swayed, reaching for the side of the wagon to steady himself. Two of the soldiers moved quickly to his side to help him.

"I think you ought to lie down, my son," Father Sacramente said. "You don't look too well. We'll take care of you. Will you help him, Carolyn?"

Burt stumbled away, being supported by the two soldiers, Carolyn walking beside them, and the priest turned back to the others.

"I don't think I've ever had a greater surprise in my life when this man turned up here and it was Colonel Sandoval."

"I came on foot about four hours ago," Sandoval told them. "When I told the villagers what was happening, they decided to move to the mountains. They wanted me to go with them, but I had told Colonel Taylor and Major Lopez I would meet them here if they were able to get across the river. I was beginning to think you weren't going to make it," he said to the two men.

"We just about didn't," Lopez said with a wry smile. "They wanted us to stay for a while. You'll be interested to know that King is a colonel in the revolutionary army."

"God bless us," Father Sacramente said. "Are you absolutely sure about that?"

"We have absolute knowledge of that fact, Father," Taylor told him with a cyn-

ical look. "We are expert witnesses."
Then he asked, "How is Xoactl?"

"Doing quite well, considering everything. After crossing the river, we rode
in a burro cart for nine or ten miles.
Then we met these four army supply
wagons from Colonel Sandoval's group.
As soon as they heard our story, they
turned around and brought us back with
them," the priest said.

"Does Xoactl know about his father's
death?" Taylor asked.

"So it is true, after all." Father Sacramente sighed. "Burt thought so, but I
kept hoping he was mistaken." The
priest paused and looked thoughtfully
toward the nearby hills. "No. I have told
the boy nothing. Perhaps there will be a
better time tomorrow. Tomorrow and tomorrow and tomorrow, when we are safe
across the border into the United
States."

"Provided that we can get across the
border, Father," Taylor said. "That is
somewhat questionable at this point."

Martinez came toward them through
the rain, juggling some tin cups in his
hands.

"Coffee, colonel?" he asked Sandoval.

"So you survived, corporal?"

"Yes, sir."

"Good. Very good. I am glad," Sandoval said.

Martinez wore a dry army coat that had every appearance of being new.

"Where did you get the clothes?" Taylor asked him.

"One of the trucks was carrying clothing and bedding supplies for Colonel Sandoval's army, sir," Martinez answered. "There is still some left if you want to check, although we unloaded most of it back there on the road to make room for the women and children."

"Women and children?" Taylor asked.

"Refugees we found on the road. We could not leave them behind for the rebels," Martinez said. Although he had not been with the trucks when these incidents happened, he had integrated himself back into his unit to the point where he spoke about the things that they did as though he had actually been part of the action.

"Bring me a map of this area, corporal," Sandoval said.

They stood on the porch of the nearest house to get out of the rain. They drank their coffee while Sandoval unfolded the map.

"Two hundred miles to the United States border and at this point only one road out...this one. The usual way to cross the river was by ferry, but now that's gone," Sandoval said.

"It may be possible to ford the river up north," Taylor said. "They can do that with their wagons."

"Do you think they'll try?" Father Sacramente asked apprehensively.

Lopez nodded. "I'm afraid so," he said. "They want the young don. King made that clear. A puppet to sit as the imperial governor in order to impress the peasants. As Colonel Sandoval says, there is only one direct route out of here. They are sure to come after us."

"Then we must keep moving," the priest said anxiously. "We have a good lead."

"Only for a time." Sandoval ran his finger along the map. "Here, seventy miles north of Sonora, is a village called Juarez. If the rebels get their hands on boats there, they can put men across the river."

"But not horses and wagons," Father Sacramente said.

"That is true. But see how the river curves to follow the valley. They would be no more than ten to twelve miles away from the road. That is no great distance for active, well-trained troops," Sandoval said.

"So you think they'll try to block the road ahead of us?" Taylor asked.

Lopez shrugged and interjected, "I don't know who their commander is, but that is what I would do if I were in his place."

"Then the sooner we get moving the better," Taylor said.

Sandoval looked up at the gray sky of the approaching evening. "We have about two hours to daylight left. We can go quite a distance in that time."

"You don't think we should push on all night?" Taylor asked.

"On this road?" Lopez laughed. "It would be suicide. Much better to camp someplace and move on at dawn. The rebels don't have any of their men across the river yet. We still have a good head start on them."

"Why don't we dump two of the wagons and just take two?" Taylor asked. "There would be room for all of us if we unload."

"I would not want to unload the ammunition," Sandoval said. "Besides, these wagons are so old we may lose a wheel or break an axle. If any of them break down, we can push on in the ones that are left."

Two of the privates had been standing listening to the conversation. As Martinez turned to move away, one of them grabbed his sleeve, and they talked low but with intensity.

Sandoval watched this for a moment and then stepped off the porch and approached them. "What is going on?" he asked.

Martinez turned. It was obvious that he was reluctant to tell the commanding officer what he had to tell him.

"Two of the men, sir, Castrol and Balaguer—they are local men. Their wives are in Sonora. They would rather stay here. They do not want to go on to the United States."

Only the drumming of the rain disturbed the silence after the corporal had finished speaking. When Taylor glanced quickly at Sandoval, he could see that the colonel's face had turned pale with anger, and the man's eyes blazed.

"For a soldier who disobeys an order in the face of the enemy, there can be only one punishment," Sandoval growled.

He drew his revolver from its holster and thumbed the hammer back. The hammer clicked ominously in the silence. "Do you understand me?" he asked.

The two men in question looked very frightened. It was obvious that they understood him. The colonel slowly lowered the hammer of the revolver and returned it to the holster.

"All right," he said. "Prepare to move out."

The men hurried away, and Father Sacramente sighed heavily. "You had me frightened, colonel," he said to Sandoval.

"That's a bad business," Lopez said. "Once such a thing starts, you can never tell where it will end. The colonel had to prevent it starting."

Sandoval nodded. "We've wasted enough time. Get things ready and we'll move out."

The native women, twelve of them, sat with five children in one of the wagons. They clutched the pathetic bundles that contained all the worldly goods they had been able to retain.

Sandoval and Lopez checked the supplies in each of the wagons. Then Sandoval looked around. "Where are Castrol and Balaguer?"

Martinez licked his lips nervously. "They have gone, my colonel."

"Did you see them go?" Sandoval demanded.

"No, sir. They were here only five minutes ago. I was talking with them."

"What about?"

"They were very angry with the colonel. They said that the rebel soldiers would catch us all, that we would never get to the United States of America." He shrugged with resignation. "They did not want to stay."

Sandoval cursed and Lopez shook his head and said, "We're better off without them, colonel. There's no problem. We have enough drivers. We can handle the wagons ourselves."

Sandoval looked at Lopez for a moment and then nodded. "Very well. I'll go in the first wagon. You follow in the next wagon, major. Father Sacramente, Miss Smith, and Xoactl Garcia can travel with you."

"Where do you want me to ride?" Taylor asked.

"You can bring up the rear with Martinez. Mr. Burt can go in the third wagon with the refugees. As soon as everyone is in, we'll move out."

As they separated, Taylor heard his name and saw Carolyn leaning out of the back of the second wagon. He climbed up on the back of the wagon beside her.

"What's happening?" she asked.

"A couple of our soldiers have deserted, but it's really nothing to worry about. How's Xoactl?"

"He's asleep right now. We've made him as comfortable as we can," she said.

The young boy was lying on some blankets in the wagon, where the supplies had been moved aside to make room. His face was pale.

"Are you worried?" Taylor asked Carolyn.

"No. Not really. I believe we can make it," she said.

He didn't know if she really believed it or was just trying to keep up her own courage, but he admired her for saying it, whatever the reason. He pulled her close to him and kissed her. She smiled at him and said nothing. They kissed again.

"I'll see you later," he told her.

He dropped down from the back of the wagon, and Father Sacramente stood there. "Would it be all right if I got in the wagon now?" the priest asked with a smile.

Taylor grinned and helped him up into

the wagon. Then he walked back to the rear wagon. Martinez was already sitting on the wagon seat, and Taylor climbed up beside him.

Sandoval walked up. "The next village is about thirty miles farther on," he said.

"We can't possibly get that far before dark," Taylor responded.

Sandoval nodded his agreement. "If we can make twelve or fifteen miles, I'll be very happy," he said. "We'll camp by the side of the road and then move on at dawn."

He moved away. Martinez had the reins in his hands, and Taylor allowed as how he would just as soon let him be the driver. The wagon in front of them started to move, and Martinez slapped the reins across the backs of their own horses.

As they followed the other wagon, Taylor suddenly felt a little better about everything. At least they weren't walking, and they were on their way toward the border. He leaned back against the board that served as a back to the wagon seat and lay the new repeating rifle he had obtained from Colonel Sandoval across his knees.

* * *

As the wagons moved out of the village, Castrol and Balaguer came out of a clump of brush and stood listening. Finally Castrol nodded in satisfaction. "They have gone," he said. "Colonel Sandoval was very angry."

"It doesn't matter," Balaguer replied. "He is finished, anyway." He looked at the smoke still rising from the chimney of a nearby house.

"There is still a fire in there. We can stay here tonight and go back to Sonora in the morning."

They went into the house, leaving the street empty. The rain pelting the roofs was the only sound in the all but deserted village of Donado.

Chapter Ten

It was getting dark and visibility was poor. The wagons slowed and Martinez guided the team off the road, following the wagon in front of them.

The place Sandoval had chosen to spend the night was a flat area with some trees between it and the road that would screen them from any chance observation.

Taylor got down from the wagon seat and walked forward while Martinez unhitched the team. Lopez, Sandoval, and Father Sacramente were standing at the rear of the second wagon, talking. Carolyn leaned out of the back of the wagon.

Sandoval turned to Taylor as he approached. "We've decided that we don't need to worry too much about the rebels seeing a fire tonight," he said. "Miss Smith has offered to oversee the cooking. We have plenty of food."

"A good hot meal should lift everyone's spirits," Father Sacramente said.

"What about the boy?" Taylor asked. "How is he doing?"

"He's all right so far," the priest said. "He's been sleeping a lot."

"What about our sleeping arrangements?" Lopez asked.

"We'll sleep in the wagons," Sandoval answered. "We'll need to take turns standing guard, of course. We'll need one guard here and one at the side of the road. I'll work out a guard-duty roster after we've eaten."

Sandoval moved away, and Father Sacramente smiled up at Carolyn. "If you'll hand me my medical bag," he said, "I'll take a look at Winston Burt."

"I'll go with you," Lopez said.

They walked away together, and Taylor helped Carolyn down out of the wagon. He saw that Martinez had finished unhitching the team and called to him.

"Miss Smith is going to cook a meal for us," Taylor told him. "Why don't you see if you can rustle up some of the drier branches around here and get a good fire going? Give her all the help that she needs."

"Yes, sir," Martinez said and moved away.

Taylor went after Father Sacramente

and Lopez. He found them in the back of
the third wagon with Winston Burt and
the women and children. A coal-oil lantern hung from the bow frame above and
lighted the interior of the covered wagon.

Burt sat quietly while Father Sacramente took the old bandages off. Burt
was pale and drawn, and every so often
he glanced nervously at Lopez, who was
watching calmly.

The priest examined Burt's arm carefully. "It isn't as bad as I thought at first.
You'll be fine in a day or so."

"It still hurts pretty bad," Burt
whined.

"My, that's sure too bad," Taylor said
from where he was perched on the back
of the wagon. "Don't you think that's too
bad, Jose?"

"It certainly is," Lopez replied with
mock solemnity. "You have to take good
care of yourself, Winston. We don't want
anything to happen to you."

Burt glared at them both with hatred.

Taylor dropped back to the ground and
walked back to where Martinez had a
fire going behind the second wagon. He
and Carolyn had the frying pan on and
were cooking potatoes and beans. A large
pot of coffee was also brewing against

the flames. Sandoval sat just inside the back of the wagon, looking at his map.

"You look worried, colonel," Taylor said.

"I'm thinking about tomorrow, Colonel Taylor. The road swings close to the river again. If the rebels have moved fast along the other side and get some men across, we could run into trouble. For example, if the bridge across the Gila Ravine was destroyed, we would not be able to get our wagons across. We would be on foot."

"Well, we can't do anything about that until tomorrow," Taylor said. "I think we should eat now."

The people from the wagons had come up now, and Martinez was kept busy passing out tin plates full of potatoes and beans. As they started to eat, Father Sacramente said to Martinez, "Will you see that Mr. Burt gets something to eat?"

Then the priest frowned at Taylor. "Weren't you a little hard on the man? Any man can lose his nerve for a little while in a situation like this."

"He never had any nerve in the first place, Father," Taylor replied sharply.

The priest frowned, glanced from Taylor to Lopez, well aware that he did not know everything that had happened, and promptly dropped the subject.

Taylor finished eating and was drinking a cup of the strong, hot coffee when Sandoval came over to him.

"I've worked out a guard roster. If you will, I'd like you to be on guard for an hour at the road starting at ten o'clock tonight. Then you'll be on duty down here for an hour starting at four in the morning. We'll all be up at five to start the day."

Taylor climbed up into the back of the wagon and lay down. He didn't need to be on duty until ten. That gave him time for a couple of hours' sleep. He closed his eyes.

It seemed to Taylor that he had just been asleep for a few minutes when someone had him by the shoulder and was shaking him. He awoke and sat up in the cold and dark.

"Yes. Okay. Okay."

Taylor pulled on his gloves. He picked up the repeating rifle, opened the back flap of the wagon, and jumped down on the wet ground. He moved through the trees to the road. At the road he stopped and called out softly. "This is Colonel Taylor."

"Okay, sir," the soldier responded.

"Anything happening?" Taylor asked.

"Nothing but this terrible weather. I hope that it doesn't turn to snow. It's cold enough."

"I hope not too," Taylor replied, and then the soldier left to head back to the wagons.

Taylor found a fallen tree and sat on it, with his rifle lying across his knees. But the cold ate into him, and from time to time he stood up and walked around to restore his circulation.

As he sat there, very gradually he became aware of the noise. He straightened up and listened carefully. He could hear the sound of feet, walking in the mud, coming from the location of the wagons. There was silence for a minute, as if the person were at a loss as to where Taylor was located, and then the steps came on again, more cautiously.

Very carefully and quietly Taylor moved to the side and worked his way around in a wide circle until he was sure he was behind the other person. Then he moved and saw the dark bulk of a man in the darkness.

It was the stillness of the man that made Taylor decide. That and the fact that the man had a rifle that was leveled. Taylor took a step forward, jabbed his rifle into the man's back, and as the other turned, Taylor hit him on the side of the head.

The man lay moaning on the ground, and Taylor struck a Lucifer match. It was Winston Burt, with his rifle lying in the mud beside him. The match hissed and then went out.

Finally Burt groaned and sat up. "What happened?" he asked, his voice quavering.

"You shouldn't go sneaking up on people like that," Taylor told him. "Someone may get the wrong idea about whose side you're on."

"I just wanted to talk to you, that's all," Burt mumbled. "I wanted to explain about what happened at Sonora. When things started to go to pieces I just panicked. I didn't know what was happening. I got to a wagon, and when no one else followed I thought that you'd all been killed."

Taylor thought that was an outright lie, but he didn't challenge it. He said, "That's okay. It's over. Those things happen."

Burt hesitated and then got slowly to his feet. "Have you told anyone else about me at Sonora?" he asked.

"No," Taylor responded. "Only Lopez and I know, and we've had other things to worry about. We're not going to say anything." He stood there for a minute, watching the other man, and then he went on, "You had better get back and get some sleep. You'll need it." He picked up the rifle and handed it to Burt. "Better take this with you."

Burt stumbled away in the dark without saying any more, and Taylor went back to sit on the fallen tree. About a half hour later Sandoval relieved him.

"Anything happen?" Sandoval asked.

"No, colonel. Everything has been quiet."

Taylor left and went back to the wagons. He climbed in the back of the wagon and lay down, pulling a blanket up over his shoulders. He was cold all over. Finally he went to sleep.

Taylor came awake slowly and turned on his side. He could hear someone outside at the rear of the wagon. He looked out of the wagon. Carolyn was crouched over the fire, watching the coffeepot.

"What time is it?" he asked softly.

She looked up at where he was looking out of the back of the wagon. "It's just after three o'clock," she answered. "I couldn't sleep."

He got out of the wagon. She poured coffee in two tin cups and handed him one. They sat in silence in the glow of the fire. After a while he asked, "What is it, Carolyn? Are you afraid?"

"I think I am," she answered simply. "Even the War of the States didn't prepare me for anything like this. Do you think we'll get out?"

He was tempted to answer with some false reassurance, and then he looked into her calm, serious face and knew that he could not.

"I'm not sure. As Colonel Sandoval says, if the rebels have moved fast along the other side, they could be ahead of us. They're bound to find some boats someplace on the river. They could put men across the river to block the road with very little trouble."

"This bridge up ahead that Colonel Sandoval mentioned—do you think that there may be trouble there?"

"There may be trouble anyplace. There's no point in our worrying too much in advance." He smiled and then changed the subject. "What are you going to do when this is over?"

"Take Xoactl to the sanitarium at

Montrose, Colorado. I promised to do that."

"And after that?" he persisted.

"I'm not sure. I don't think the Army has as much need for nurses now, with no war going on."

"Isn't it about time you thought about settling down?" he asked.

"Is this a marriage proposal?" she countered quickly.

He shook his head. "I'm doing pretty well financially, Carolyn," he said. "But look at the negative side. I'm almost forty years old—an old, washed-up, ready-to-retire soldier who's been too many places and seen too many things. I want to rest for a while. That doesn't sound like much of a catch for a young woman."

"If we don't try," she told him quietly, "we'll be sorry the rest of our lives."

He sat staring into the fire. Finally he sighed and stood up. "I'm going to walk for a minute before my guard turn. I have some thinking to do."

Carolyn sat in the darkness. In a few minutes Lopez walked up. He poured himself a cup of coffee and squatted down on the other side of the fire from her.

"I should wake Ford," he said. "He's

supposed to relieve me at four o'clock for guard duty."

"He's awake," she said. "He was just here. He's gone for a walk so he could think."

"Anything wrong?" Lopez asked.

Carolyn shrugged and smiled faintly. "Four-o'clock-in-the-morning talk is all. He was just telling me that he's too old for me."

Lopez nodded without smiling and sipped his coffee. "He's just tired, that's all," he said. Then he hesitated for a minute before he decided to go on. "Ford wouldn't particularly want me to tell you this, Carolyn, but for the past while, ever since he supposedly was put out to pasture here by the Army, he has been working for the United States Government Intelligence. Mainly out West here, making trips into Mexico to try to stay in touch with the situation here. The man named Ferre is his Washington contact."

Carolyn looked at him closely. She was obviously surprised. "Are you sure about this?" she asked.

"Oh, yes," he answered. "I know it for a fact. It's a long time for a man to live on his nerves."

"That explains a lot of things," she said.

He nodded and leaned closer to her across the small fire, so his voice could not carry and be heard by anyone else.

"He's a very good man, Carolyn. But he ought to quit this kind of thing. When this is over, take him home. Wherever you want home to be."

She smiled. She was relaxed and happy now that she had this new information. "Thank you, Jose. I appreciate it. I'll do just what you said." She stood up. "I'd better go check on Xoactl."

Lopez poured himself another cup of coffee. He sat by the fire, and in just a few minutes Taylor joined him.

"Where's Carolyn?" he asked.

"Gone to check on Xoactl. Who's guarding up on the road?"

"Martinez, I think." Taylor hesitated a minute, then he went on, "Burt came up there when I was on guard last night."

"What did he want?"

"I'm not really sure. I had an idea that maybe he was thinking of killing me. What he apparently wanted was to make sure that we hadn't told anyone else what happened with him at Sonora."

He told Jose what had happened. When he finished, Lopez nodded, a frown on his face.

"Of course," Lopez said, "he would say

that he was carrying the gun in case of trouble. It would have been far too noisy to shoot you. If he had been going to kill you, he should have gone after you with a knife."

"I don't know that the man is sane enough to reason things out that way," Taylor said. "He's really scared, and I don't know that he has the kind of courage that it takes to go after another man with a knife."

"Well, we'll have to watch him more carefully," Lopez said. "I don't like it. We don't need that kind of thing in our own camp." He laughed strangely. "I must be getting old."

"Aren't we all?" Taylor said. "I've been thinking myself that I'm far too old to keep on with this kind of thing. After this trip I really think I may retire from the Army."

Wrapped in a blanket on the floor of the hut back at Donado, Castrol was suddenly awakened by a kick in the ribs. He sat up with a start, suddenly aware of faces staring at him and of the many men dressed in the uniforms of the rebels, and they were holding rifles.

Colonel King stood in the doorway, his

collar pulled up around his face. He was obviously tired.

There had been a delay in getting his men across the river. They had lost one wagon in the heavy waters, and he had decided to continue on with just one wagon and a dozen men.

They had ridden most of the night, but they had kept on in the hope that Father Sacramente and his party might be at Donado. When they had reached the village, he had sent his sergeant and ten men in on foot. Then in five minutes he had followed the man in the wagon.

"What's going on here?" he asked.

The sergeant spoke up. "The village is empty, colonel, except for these two. Apparently they are deserters."

"Deserters?" King's face took on a look of excitement. "Who are you?" he asked Castrol. "One of Diego Sandoval's men? Did you escape across the river?"

"No, sir," Castrol said. "I was with the supply wagons."

"The supply wagons were here?" King said, animation in his voice. "Where are they now"

"Gone, sir, toward the United States with Colonel Sandoval and Xoactl Garcia. They are hoping to reach the border."

"Diego Sandoval was here?" King asked in amazement.

"Oh, yes, sir," Castrol babbled. "Also Major Lopez and the United States colonel called Taylor. They all crossed the river from Sonora."

"When did they leave?" King asked.

"Yesterday. Two hours before dark. They were going to camp somewhere along the road when night came. I heard Colonel Sandoval say so."

King laughed with excitement. "Get your men together, sergeant," he said. "We're going to move on."

King started for the door, and the sergeant asked him, "What shall we do with those two men, sir?"

King shrugged. "We have no further need of them," he said.

He turned and went out the door. As he went down the steps to the muddy road, there were two loud rifle shots from within the house.

Chapter Eleven

"I can see the bridge," Colonel Sandoval said, "and it's still standing."

"I'm grateful for that," Taylor said and took the binoculars from Sandoval. "There doesn't seem to be anyone about."

"And there's no place they can ambush us from," Lopez said. "We'd better get across now while we can."

They moved back to the wagons, and Taylor swung up onto the seat beside Martinez. At least there was some cover from the wagon top so that he could get out of the terrible weather. The rain was still continuing to fall.

They moved up over the hill, and the road dropped steeply toward the great ravine, which cut its way through the mountains like a miniature Grand Canyon. They held back on the reins, to keep the horses from going too fast, and the wagons moved cautiously.

The bridge was narrow and rickety looking. As the road leveled off to approach it, the wagons all slowed to a halt and Martinez stopped the team.

"I'll go see what's happening," Taylor said and jumped down off the wagon.

Sandoval was leaning over the edge, looking at the bridge. As Taylor approached him, he turned and said, "It would take the rebels a long time to build another bridge here. It's a dynamite man's dream."

"Are you thinking of doing it yourself?" Taylor asked.

"I don't see why not. It wouldn't take long. We'll cross over and then blast it so no one can follow."

As Taylor walked back to his wagon, Martinez was leaning over from the seat. "What's he up to, sir?" Martinez asked.

"He wants to stop and dynamite the bridge. What do you think about that?" Taylor asked him.

"I think it's a great idea, sir. It would block the road for a long time."

"Don't you think it would let the rebels know that we're here?" Taylor asked.

"I don't think it makes any difference. If there's anyone up ahead of us, they'll still be there whether we blow up the bridge or not."

Taylor climbed up beside Martinez, and the wagon moved forward and crossed the bridge with the others. They all moved a little way beyond the bridge and then stopped in a line on the road. Taylor and Martinez got down and moved forward as Burt's wagon drove up behind.

Burt walked forward from his wagon. His face was white, and Taylor thought it showed a great deal of strain.

"Why are we stopping now?" Burt demanded.

"I have decided to dynamite the bridge before we go on," Sandoval said.

Father Sacramente climbed down to join them, and Carolyn stayed in the wagon, her arm around Xoactl Garcia, who was now sitting up beside her.

"For heaven's sake!" Burt exploded. "Haven't we lost enough time already?"

"If we destroy this bridge, the rebels will lose even more time," Sandoval said. "There are boxes of dynamite in my wagon. We'll take it back to the bridge and then drive the other wagons farther up the road. If we all help, it won't take long."

They moved three of the wagons farther on and took the colonel's wagon right back to the middle of the bridge. Taylor and Lopez climbed into the back of the wagon and handed the boxes and dynamite, blasting caps, and fuse out to the others. Finally they were finished.

"What now?" Lopez asked.

"I'll fix the fuse myself," Sandoval said. "The two privates can stay and help me. The rest of you better get back up the hill. You'll have to walk. We'll keep the wagon here so we can get away faster when we light the fuse."

One of the privates stood, staring at the colonel, the fear obvious in his face. Sandoval threw him a coil of fuse.

"Pull yourself together, soldier," he snapped. "The sooner we get this done, the sooner we can get away."

The rest of them moved out on foot quickly. At the top of the hill, Taylor and Lopez stopped and looked back down on the bridge. Lopez had Sandoval's binoculars. He sat on a rock and adjusted them.

"How are they doing?" Taylor asked him.

"The colonel is setting the dynamite," Lopez answered. "The two soldiers do not look too happy."

"They're both scared to death," Taylor said. "And I think that's exactly why Colonel Sandoval made them stay."

The men below on the bridge worked rapidly. Suddenly one of the soldiers pointed and shouted as a wagon load of soldiers came over the hill on the far side of the ravine. Lopez looked up and focused the binoculars on the officer sitting on the wagon seat beside the driver.

"It's King!" he said.

As the wagon with the rebel troops in it started down the hill toward the bridge, Taylor said, "They don't have time to blow the bridge up now. We'd better get moving."

"Their wagon would catch us in a short time, anyway," Lopez said calmly. "Colonel Sandoval knows that. He'll stay and blow up the bridge. He'll do it for Xoactl and Don Garcia."

Taylor stood and watched what was happening on the bridge below. He saw Sandoval walk toward the place where the dynamite was set, and he knew that Lopez was right. The colonel intended to blow up the bridge even if it meant that he would go up with it.

One of the privates on the bridge rushed at the colonel and hit him on the back of the head. Sandoval staggered and fell to his knees. Then the two soldiers ran for the wagon.

Sandoval reached into his pocket and brought out a Lucifer match. He struck it and when it lighted, he held it against the fuse right at the point where the fuse entered the blasting cap and the stick of dynamite.

At that moment the two soldiers lashed the horses, and the wagon lurched into motion. It had moved about five yards when the middle of the bridge erupted in a cloud of fire and smoke. Pieces of wood were thrown into the air as a series of violent explosions occurred one right after the other, and then the entire bridge collapsed, the wagon going down into the ravine with the two soldiers, Sandoval, and the pieces of the bridge.

The troop wagon had stopped on the other side of the ravine, and the troops jumped out and began firing their rifles at the wagons on the other side.

Burt jumped up onto the seat of the wagon carrying the women and children and slapped the reins across the backs of the horses. Lopez drove the wagon carrying Father Sacramente, Carolyn, and Xoactl, and Martinez and Taylor followed in the third wagon.

Bullets hit the dirt around them for a few seconds, and then they were out of range of the rifle fire. They kept going for a while longer, and then all three wagons stopped in the road.

Lopez and Taylor got down from their

wagons, and Burt stumbled toward them, his face distorted and looking like that of a wild man.

"What are we going to do now?" he almost screamed.

Lopez ignored him and held up Sandoval's map. "At least Colonel Sandoval left us this," he said.

"He was a good man," Taylor said sadly. "He did what a good soldier should do."

Lopez spread the map out, and they looked at it.

"I thought so," Lopez said. "There is another village about ten or twelve miles farther on. Then we are only about forty miles from the border."

"That's as the crow flies?" Taylor asked with wry humor.

"Or as the crow laboriously plods along the mountain trails," Lopez answered in the same vein.

They had been through an emotional experience, and now they had to ease their tensions by some light banter that might not have fit in with what had been happening, but it was necessary for them.

"One thing is certain," Taylor said. "King can't hope to catch us now."

Lopez nodded and looked back at the

map. "I hope you're right. As long as there are no rebels waiting at the next village, we should be all right. But we can never be sure."

"What about leaving a couple of these wagons and traveling lighter?" Taylor asked.

Lopez shook his head. "If anything went wrong with the wagon we were traveling in, we would really be in trouble. There's another advantage—three wagons give us a little more of a show of strength. That might be helpful if we run into any small rebel patrols."

"What about these women and children?" Burt interrupted. "Don't you think it's time that we left them?"

"For the rebels to get their hands on?" Lopez said. "Even for someone like you, that isn't such a great idea, Burt. Get back to your wagon and take up the last position."

Burt turned and headed back to his wagon, looking as if he had been hit.

"Go easy, major," Father Sacramente remonstrated. "You can see that the man is just about at the end of his rope."

"Which is the reason he has to be driven, Father," Lopez replied firmly.

Then Lopez turned to Taylor. "You and Martinez take the lead in your wagon,

Ford, and I'll follow. If there is any trouble, try to block the road with your wagon. That will give us a chance to turn around. Then you can leave your wagon and run back and get in with us."

"I certainly hope that I can," Taylor replied with a wry grin.

He waved to Carolyn and she waved back. So did Xoactl. It was the first real sign of life that Taylor had noticed from the boy.

Taylor climbed up onto the wagon seat beside Martinez. He leaned back against the backboard of the seat with the rifle across his lap. They set out and had been bumping along the rutted road for about fifteen minutes when Lopez's wagon came up closer behind them and he shouted at them. Martinez pulled the team to a halt, and Lopez got down from his wagon and walked up to them.

"Burt doesn't seem to be following us," Lopez said.

"I wonder what the fool is up to now," Taylor said.

"As far as he is concerned, I'd leave him," Lopez said, "but we have to think of the women and children."

Taylor nodded and looked back down the trail. There was no sign of anyone. "You wait here, Jose. Martinez and I will go back in our wagon. Maybe he's just had a breakdown of his wagon."

Martinez maneuvered the team around, and they went back up the road. It was just a few minutes until they saw the wagon pulled over to the side of the erstwhile road, with Burt and the women standing beside it. Martinez turned the wagon around, and he and Taylor got out and walked back.

"I'm glad you came back," Burt said, and his nervousness was very apparent.

"What happened?" Taylor asked.

"One of the wagon's wheels locked," Burt answered. "I don't know if the axle is broken or the hub is stuck or what."

"We certainly didn't need this," Taylor said.

"Now we'll have to leave these women," Burt said, almost eagerly.

Taylor gave him a withering look and then deliberately turned back to Martinez. "Take a look underneath, corporal," he said.

In a few minutes Martinez called to him. He pushed his way through the group of women and crawled under the wagon in the mud beside Martinez.

"There's a very large stick pushed in between the axle and the wheel here, sir," Martinez said. "It looks to me like it was done deliberately."

As they tugged at the stick to pull it out, they could hear a shout and the other wagon started off. Taylor scrambled out from under the wagon, but Burt was already headed down the road in the other wagon and was urging the horses onward in a gallop.

Martinez crawled out from the wagon and moved up alongside Taylor. "There are several appropriate punishments I could think of for people like Mr. Burt," Martinez said softly, "but I wouldn't mention them in front of a group of women. What do we do now, sir?"

"We'll have to take this wagon and go after him," Taylor said. Then he turned to the women. "Come on, everyone. Get back in the wagon and we'll go on. Hurry, please!"

Taylor had no idea what Burt would do when he reached Lopez and the other wagon—probably just keep right on going. And there was no way of knowing what Lopez would do. Taylor thought they had better catch Burt as soon as they could.

He climbed up onto the wagon seat, with Martinez sitting on his right. When all of the women were back in the wagon, Taylor slapped the reins and shouted to the horses. The wagon started off down the road.

"That one wheel is grabbing," Taylor said to Martinez. "I hope that Winston Burt didn't do any permanent damage jamming that stick in there."

"Let's hope not, sir."

Within about five minutes they came to the place where they had left Lopez and the wagon with the others. There were the tracks of the two wagons, but nothing else to mark the place. Taylor didn't think this was a good sign, but there was nothing to do but to continue on. He didn't like to push the team any harder or faster. Doing that would not be good for the horses, and also he was concerned about the one wagon wheel.

The road went along the valley floor for a while, and then it began to lift up along the side of the mountains, heading for the pass that would take them across the border into the United States.

Taylor guided the team carefully along the road as it cut up the mountainside. The wheel kept grabbing, and Taylor wondered how long it would be before it came off completely. That kind of thing did happen with wagons, and he had no grease with which to lubricate the wheel or the axle.

He rounded a curve and came to the crest of a hill, and the road dropped sharply into the valley below. He leaned over and looked past Martinez. There was no sign of the other two wagons. There was only the rain-soaked edge of the road, and the mountain dropped steeply for what looked to be a couple of hundred feet below.

The wagon started down the descent, skidding with a sickening lurch. Taylor was trembling and Martinez was pale and sweating beside him. The wagon jerked as Taylor negotiated a curve in the road. The damaged wheel grabbed, and the wagon skidded toward the edge. Taylor yelled at the horses and tried to urge them forward faster to pull the wagon from the edge.

But the horses couldn't get a firm footing on the muddy road, and instead of their pulling the wagon, the wagon began pulling the horses toward the edge. It lurched again, and the back went over the edge.

"Jump for it!" Taylor yelled at the top of his voice.

He dove out of the wagon head first, landing flat on his face in the mud of the road. The wagon hung on the edge for a brief second, but Martinez was on the side that went over first, and he could not fight his way clear. The wagon went over the side, with screams from the women and children trapped inside. There was a terrible crunching, shattering noise as the wagon, the horses, and the people all fell to the bottom of the rocky gulch below.

Taylor lay in the mud. He was sick and weak, emotionally drained from what had just happened. Unfortunately, there was nothing that he could do to help the poor individuals who had plunged to the valley below. They were beyond help. He didn't even want to go to the edge and look down, because he knew that what he had to see would not be a pleasant sight, and that would not bring anyone back to life.

Finally he got unsteadily to his feet and struggled upright. He felt sick to his stomach, but he knew he had to move on. He started walking down the muddy roadway. For a half a mile the road dropped steeply down toward the valley. The rain felt colder to Taylor, and darkness started to fall.

He knew there was only one way to go. He had no choice. And now he wasn't even armed. His rifle had gone down into the valley with the wagon. Slowly the rain was beginning to change to snow.

Down the road ahead of him he heard the sound of rifle fire. He didn't know if it was Lopez, Burt, or the rebels. Things were starting to look desperate. If he stayed on the road, he was obviously going to run into trouble. And if he didn't find some shelter, he might even freeze to death on a night like this.

Then he could hear the sound of horses' hooves on the road ahead. Quickly he moved off the road into the underbrush. He stepped behind a tree and waited.

Four horsemen rode by. Taylor could tell by the way the men were dressed that they were members of the rebel army, and they had rifles slung over their shoulders.

"What do I do now?" he mumbled out loud after the horsemen had passed by.

There was a soft chuckle right behind him, and Major Jose Lopez said, "That's exactly what I was wondering."

Chapter Twelve

"When I first heard you coming down the road, I thought there was trouble," Lopez said. "When those revolutionaries rode by and you ducked into the woods, I knew it was you."

Taylor reached out and took hold of his friend's hand in sheer relief. "Jose, you old son of a gun! What happened?"

"You tell me. We were waiting for you to come back when you went after Burt. Then your wagon went by like a bat out of the dark regions, like the whole rebel army was after you."

"That was Burt, not me," Taylor said, and then he explained quickly what had happened, including the loss of the people and the wagon.

There was a moment's silence when he finished, and then Lopez said, "There has been heavy firing on the road up ahead. I think he may have paid the price already, Ford."

"He couldn't," Taylor said grimly. "The price is far too high."

"Perhaps. But ever since Sonora I'm not sure that Winston Burt has really been responsible for all of his actions," Lopez said philosophically.

"Where's your wagon?" Taylor asked, abruptly changing the subject.

"About fifty yards back in the woods. I left the road when we heard the firing up ahead. I came back to make sure that our tracks were covered."

"Judging from the soldiers," Taylor said, "the next village is obviously in the hands of the revolutionaries. What are we going to do?"

Lopez shook his head. "I don't have an idea. We'll discuss it in more uncomfortable surroundings. I think we'll be safe here for the night."

Taylor followed him through the darkness, and the wagon loomed up in the night.

"Look out for the supplies," Lopez said. "I dumped a lot of the things out of the wagon."

The canvas curtain at the back of the wagon moved slightly, and Father Sacramente said softly, "Major Lopez?"

"And friend," Lopez replied. "I've found our missing person."

Taylor followed him, and they climbed up into the back of the wagon. There was a coal-oil lantern that lit up the inside. Father Sacramente sat on one side, but Taylor only had eyes for Carolyn Smith, who was seated on the other side of the wagon, next to Xoactl.

"Oh, Ford!" she whispered.

He moved closer to her and took her hands in his. He just looked at her and said nothing. Then he touched his lips to her hand.

"What happened?" she asked softly.

He told the story again, quickly. There were tears in her eyes when he finished.

"Those poor, poor women," she said, "and the children and Corporal Martinez too."

"There wasn't anything I could do, Carolyn," Taylor said. "There just wasn't anything."

"I didn't think we'd make it over that mountain ourselves," Lopez said.

There was silence for a period of time in the wagon. Then Father Sacramente said slowly, "The shooting we heard earlier, then—it must have been Winston Burt?"

Lopez nodded in agreement. "There

were rebels on horseback on the road. That means they must be in control of the next village."

"Are we safe here?" the priest asked.

"For tonight," Lopez answered.

"And in the morning?" the priest persisted.

Lopez shrugged and avoided looking directly at the old man. "I don't really know. Even if we can get the wagon out of these woods, we have no place to go. We'd never get through the next village, and we all know that King can't be far behind us. At least we have shelter and food here," he finished, somewhat lamely.

"Beans," Carolyn told Taylor. "Coffee and beans."

"Better than nothing," Taylor said, grinning.

Carolyn handed him a tin cup of coffee, and Xoactl smiled at him.

Taylor smiled back at the boy. "This type of living seems to have helped Xoactl," he said. "He's better than he was before."

Taylor stared at the lantern, remembering Xoactl's father, Don Garcia, and the grim circumstances of his death. Then he thought about King. In a sense, they had been friends. It was strange how the world turned and how things turned out. He finished the coffee and handed the cup back to Carolyn.

"Do you still have the map, Jose?" Taylor asked.

Lopez pulled it out of his pocket and spread it out on the wooden bed of the wagon.

"How far are we from the village?" Taylor asked.

"Here. Right close by," Lopez said, pointing. "It's called Pascale. The United States border is roughly forty miles beyond."

Taylor looked at the map closely. "Look," he said, "there's a trail that goes up the mountain from the village. There's a place up on top of the plateau."

"Mission Escalante," Father Sacramente said. "It's an old Catholic mission that was built before this road was even put here. People used to stay overnight there when they came over this pass. I have heard about it, but I've never been there."

Lopez looked at the map. "That's a pretty high elevation, Ford. With the snow starting, we would never make it over there on foot."

"The two of you could make it across

the pass with the boy," Father Sacramente said.

"We could *all* make it if we were on horses," Taylor said.

"Horses?" Lopez frowned. "We've got the two that were pulling the wagon, but they're not too good for riding. And there are only two. We ought to have at least two more."

"Like you said," Taylor went on, "the village is right close. If we slipped in before dawn, we shouldn't have much trouble getting a couple of horses."

"Just you and I could go into the village," Lopez agreed. "The others can wait for us here. When we get back, we can cut across the mountain to the trail that leads to the mission. That is, if we come back with the horses."

"At least it's a chance," Taylor said. "Can you think of anything better?"

"Unfortunately, Ford, I can't. It's about as good a plan as any. At least it will give us some kind of a chance."

"Then I suggest that we get some sleep," Taylor said. "We're going to need it."

He wrapped himself in a blanket and lay down next to Lopez and Father Sacramente. On the other side of the wagon bed, Carolyn Smith slept with her arm around the young boy.

Taylor slept well in spite of the cold and the hard wooden wagon bed on which he was lying. When he got up and climbed out of the back of the wagon, it was still dark. There was some snow on the ground, but not as much as he had expected. He built a fire, and when he had finished getting it going Carolyn joined him. She stood close and took hold of his hand.

"We'll get there, Ford. I know we will," she told him.

"We have to keep believing that," he said. "Why don't you start the coffee brewing and I'll wake Jose?"

Lopez stuck his head out of the back of the wagon. "No need. I'm awake. What's the day like?"

Taylor shrugged. "It could be worse. It didn't snow a lot."

"There'll be more," Lopez said. "We had better get ready to go."

Father Sacramente came from the wagon and joined them. "How are you, Father?" Taylor asked.

"I'm feeling my age, but I'll manage."

"One thing I didn't ask last night," Lopez said. "Can you ride?"

Carolyn nodded as he looked at her. "We had horses when I was back home," she said. "I've ridden since I was a child."

The priest indicated that he had had some experience riding, but it had been a while.

Lopez gave Taylor another repeating rifle from the supplies in the wagon, and they each filled their pockets with a supply of bullets. Then they quickly ate a breakfast of coffee and beans.

Lopez and Taylor had decided to walk into the village rather than take the two horses that had been pulling the wagon. The horses were not riding horses, and they wanted to leave them with the wagon so that if they didn't return, Father Sacramente, Carolyn, and Xoactl would at least have a fighting chance of getting away.

When all the preparations had been made, Taylor looked at Lopez. "Are you ready?"

"If one can ever be said to be ready for this kind of thing," Lopez answered.

Together they moved away from the wagon. In the gloom of early dawn Carolyn and Father Sacramente were as shadows as they left.

"We'll be back in a couple of hours," Taylor said, trying to sound confident.

* * *

The two men walked down the road, staying to the side so as not to be obvious to anyone who might happen to come along.

"I'm afraid we left too late," Lopez said. "It's going to be light before we get to the village."

He was right. The sky was showing definite signs of the early-morning light. They hurried along the rutted road. Suddenly Lopez, who was in the lead, put up a hand and stopped. Taylor moved quietly up beside him. There, pulled a ways back into the woods, was the other wagon. They stood for a minute, and then they moved forward slowly.

The canvas of the wagon was torn, and there were bullet holes splintered into the wooden sides.

"It looks like he ran right into the middle of them," Lopez said.

The horses had been unhitched and taken away; apparently they had not been killed. The two men looked in the back of the wagon, but there was nothing. Then Lopez moved to the far side and called to Taylor.

The body of Winston Burt was sprawled in the brush by the side of the wagon. There were several ragged, bloody holes in his chest.

They stood looking down at the body, and then suddenly they heard the sound of horses' hooves. Lopez and Taylor were hidden from the road by the wagon. Along the road two mounted rebel soldiers came riding, their rifles slung on their backs.

"We can't let them go on," Lopez whispered urgently, "or they'll come upon the other wagon."

They quickly readied their rifles as the two Mexican rebel soldiers rode up to the wagon. Lopez rested his rifle against the trunk of a tree, and the two riders had just reined up when he fired the first shot and tumbled the first horseman out of his saddle.

The second rider frantically fought to turn his horse and get away. He was still jerking at the reins when two rifle bullets lifted him from the saddle.

Taylor and Lopez immediately ran forward and grabbed the reins of the two horses. They swung up into the saddles and were starting back up the road when Lopez looked down on the road that was winding up from the village.

"There are more horsemen coming up

from the village," he said. "They must have started out early this morning."

The two of them kicked the horses into a gallop and headed back up the road. When they got to where the other wagon was hidden in the woods, they turned off the road. Taylor noticed that the wagon wasn't nearly as well hidden in the stark light of morning as it had seemed at night.

Father Sacramente was standing beside the wagon as they rode up. "What happened?" he asked.

"We'll tell you later," Taylor said. "We've got to run for it. Get Xoactl."

Carolyn passed the boy out of the back of the wagon, his pale face peeking out from the blanket she had wrapped around him. Then she climbed out of the wagon, holding the priest's medical bag. Taylor dismounted and helped her mount up into the saddle. Then he handed her the boy. She settled him on the horse in front of her, and Taylor handed her the reins.

"Go across the road and up the hillside," he said, "and hurry!"

Lopez was helping Father Sacramente into the saddle when they heard the sound of horses and voices from down the road.

Taylor levered a cartridge into the magazine of his rifle and yelled, "Get out of here, Jose! I'll hold them off!"

Lopez did not argue. He leaped onto the horse behind the priest and slapped the horse's rump with his open palm. It leaped forward, and the other horse followed close behind.

Taylor ran from the wagon and got behind a large tree, steadying his rifle against the trunk. He could hear the two horses moving off through the woods.

A mounted rebel soldier burst through the trees toward the wagon, another riding right behind him. Taylor fired several shots as rapidly as he could work the lever of the rifle. Both men and horses went down in a confused heap. Taylor turned then and ran through the trees, following the trail in the snow left by his friends. There was sudden movement to his right, and he fired several shots in that general direction and ran on.

As he ran into a small clearing, a rebel soldier ran out of the trees on his right. Taylor's rifle was empty. He threw it at the soldier and ran at the man at the same headlong pace.

The man dodged the gun and tried to aim his own, but he could not do it in time. Taylor grabbed at the man's throat and quickly drove his knee into his groin. As the rebel soldier sank to the ground, Taylor hit him with a hard right fist, grabbed the man's rifle, and ran.

Taylor gasped for air as he stumbled through the trees. Several soldiers were running toward him, but they weren't cavalry; they were foot soldiers. And then he suddenly saw Colonel King in his long uniform coat.

Taylor emptied the rifle in the general direction of the soldiers and King. Then he ran across the road and started to scramble up the hillside.

The man behind him yelled and fired and started running after him. As he went up the hill, there was an explosion between him and the soldiers. Then there was another explosion. Taylor kept moving up the hill, and then he fell. Someone dragged him up to his feet, and Lopez said,"A good thing I brought those two sticks of dynamite with me."

Taylor leaned against him and gasped for breath. "Those rebels I ran in to now," he said, "they weren't soldiers from the village—they were King and his men. Isn't he ever going to give up?"

"I doubt it." Lopez grinned and slapped him on the shoulder. "We'd better get moving. King will need horses if he's going to follow us. That will take time. Maybe with any luck one of those sticks of dynamite killed him off."

Then they saw the soldiers below them at the foot of the hill. Those that weren't dead were struggling to their feet. One man stood straight and tall, wearing a long uniform coat.

"No such luck," Taylor said and then he cursed.

Taylor and Lopez turned and walked up the hill into the falling snow.

Down on the road, Colonel King turned to examine the dead and the dying. There were only four men left on their feet, and then one of the soldiers from the village limped out of the woods, clutching his bloody arm.

King walked to meet him. "You are from the village?" he asked.

"Yes, colonel."

"How did you get there?"

"By boat from Juarez, sir. Two patrols crossed over, and we came down the river."

"Are there horses at the village?"

"As many as you may need, colonel."

King took out his map and looked over it. He traced his finger along the trail leading up over the mountain to Mission Escalante.

"So that's where they're going," he said softly to the sergeant.

"I think that is a mission up there, sir. An old Spanish mission."

King folded the map up and turned to the wounded soldier. "How far is the village?" he asked.

"Less than five miles, colonel."

"Then we have no time to waste." King nodded to the sergeant. "We'll walk there as quickly as possible and get horses."

"And what about the wounded here, colonel?"

"Leave them. We'll send someone back from the village to get them."

He turned and started to walk along the road in the falling snow.

Chapter Thirteen

The hillside was rough and rocky, and the light blanket of snow had made the footing unsure. Major Lopez led the way, walking. He was followed by Father Sacramente on one horse and Carolyn and Xoactl on the other. Colonel Taylor followed on foot.

"How are you doing?" Taylor asked Carolyn.

"I'm fine. So is Xoactl," she replied, looking down at him.

"Do you think we can find the trail?" Taylor called out to Lopez.

"I'm sure we can. If we keep climbing in a diagonal direction, we can't miss it."

They struggled on up the mountainside, fighting against the storm and the roughness of the terrain. It was the snow on the ground that finally showed them the trail, zigzagging up the steep slope.

They followed the trail upward, and it led through a ravine, where the mountains on either side gave them a rest from the buffeting of the wind and the driving snow. Then the trail led out onto a plateau and leveled out.

Lopez stopped at that point and took hold of the bridle of Father Sacramente's horse.

"I think we should rest here for a while," he said.

Carolyn handed Xoactl down to Taylor, and then she swung down off the horse.

"How is the boy?" Lopez asked.

"He's sleeping," Carolyn said. "He's taking this better than any of the rest of us."

"Do you have my medical bag, my dear?" Father Sacramente asked her.

She unhooked the bag from the saddle horn and carried it to where he was sitting on a rock. "Can I help you find something?" she asked.

"No," he said, smiling. "I can find it myself."

Carolyn took the canvas water bag off the saddle. She had filled it with coffee before they left that morning. It was obviously cold, but she thought it might give them some stimulation and some lift. As they passed it around and took turns drinking from it, the old priest took a small corked bottle from the medical bag, uncorked it, and sipped some of the contents.

Carolyn looked at him with a question in her eyes.

"I have a bit of a heart condition," he explained. "Some of the modern medical people think that nitroglycerine is effective in treating the heart. I have been taking a little bit of it, and it does seem to help."

"Nitroglycerine!" Taylor exclaimed. "That's what they use in dynamite."

"That's true," Father Sacramente agreed. "But if it can treat an old heart like mine, I'm willing to try it."

He sipped some of the coffee, and Taylor and Lopez moved away from the others.

"The priest doesn't look good," Taylor said. "How long will it be until we reach the mission?"

"Two or three hours," Lopez answered. "It all depends on the condition of the trail."

"How do we know anyone is going to be there when we get there?" Taylor asked. "There are many old, abandoned Catholic missions all over Mexico."

"At least we'll find some kind of shelter," Lopez said. "And we can use that as soon as possible. Neither the old man nor the boy, nor even Carolyn, can last very long in these conditions."

The two of them moved back to the others, and Father Sacramente struggled to his feet. The nitroglycerine must have done some good because he looked a lot better.

He smiled at them. "I can move out whenever you're ready, gentlemen."

Lopez helped him mount up, and after Carolyn got into the saddle, Taylor handed the boy up to her. Then they moved on. Lopez and Taylor held on to the bridles of the two horses now and walked just ahead to make sure that the horses did not bolt and run, and to keep them on the trail.

Taylor could tell that Carolyn was near exhaustion, but every time he looked up at her, she managed to smile down at him. He smiled back, trying to be reassuring.

They led the horses along the trail, and finally the ground in the mountainous area seemed to flatten out ahead of them.

"This is the main plateau," Lopez called back. "The mission can't be far now."

They moved up over a small hill, and there, perched on a rise in the plateau, stood the Mission Escalente. It wasn't large and it seemed, from here, to be deserted.

Lopez urged the horse on, and Taylor followed behind them. They moved into the area in front of the main building, and Taylor held the bridles of both horses while Lopez went up to the huge wooden door with the large, carved cross fastened to the front.

He tried the door, but it did not open. Then he beat on the wood with his open palm. He was almost becoming desperate when he heard the sound of a wooden bolt being drawn back, and the door swung open.

A Catholic monk stood there in a brown robe. He smiled at them.

"I am Father Juan Chavez," he said. "Welcome."

Taylor and Lopez helped Father Sacramente, Carolyn, and Xoactl down off the horses, and they were ushered into the building. A younger monk came out, and Taylor and Lopez followed him with their horses. They went around the back where the stables were. The young monk indicated that he would take care of the horses and directed them into the main building through the back door.

They walked along a narrow corridor

and entered a large, mostly bare room, where a fire burned in a fireplace at the end. Carolyn sat on a bench in front of the fire, holding Xoactl in her arms. Father Sacramente sat on a bench beside a large wooden table, talking to the monk.

"I've been telling Father Chavez about some of our misfortunes and problems," Father Sacramente said. "Fortunately for us, there are still some monks who tend this mission."

"Can we stay here for a while?" Taylor asked.

"Certainly, my son. As long as you wish," the elderly monk said.

"Has Father Sacramente told you that we are being followed by rebel troops?" Taylor went on.

The monk nodded. "Sound travels well here in the mountains. We could hear you coming for quite a distance. We will hear anything following you in plenty of time. I have someone bringing food and blankets to you. I suggest that you try to get some sleep."

"That is the best suggestion I've heard for a long time," Lopez said.

Father Chavez left the room, and soon one of the young monks brought a large bowl of hot food and blankets. They ate and then Carolyn, Xoactl, and Father

Sacramente wrapped up in blankets and lay down on the stone floor in front of the fire.

Lopez spread the map out on the table, and Taylor looked over his shoulder.

"Where do we go now?" Taylor asked.

Lopez traced the trail with his finger, following it down the other side of the mountain. "About twelve or fifteen miles to the United States border from here."

Taylor looked over at the three people sleeping in front of the fireplace. "Do you think they can make it?"

Lopez shrugged rather resignedly. "They'll have to," he said. "There just isn't any other choice."

He folded the map up, took a blanket, wrapped it around himself, and joined the other three on the floor in front of the fire.

Taylor sat at the table and stared at the flickering flames in the old stone fireplace. He sat that way for a long time, just thinking. Finally he merely put his head down on his folded arms on the table and dropped off to sleep sitting up.

Taylor awakened suddenly, his arms numb from his lying on them. As he looked around, he was aware of Father Chavez standing inside the doorway.

"How long have I been asleep?" Taylor asked softly.

The monk came and sat on the bench across the table from him. "About three hours," he answered. "It is the night."

Taylor looked over at the small group sleeping on the floor beside the fire. "They are very tired. They've been through a great ordeal."

The old monk nodded sympathetically. "I understand," he said. "And I hate to add to your burden."

Taylor looked up at him quickly and questioningly.

"They are coming," Father Chavez said simply.

"Are you sure?"

The monk nodded. Then he said, "They are crossing the plateau even as we speak."

"Is there any place you could hide us?" Taylor asked him.

The monk shook his head. "The mission is small. Since they are looking for you, they will search everywhere."

Taylor moved over to the fireplace and took hold of Lopez's shoulder. The major was immediately awake.

"Trouble?" he asked.

"Yes," Taylor said. "King and his men

are not too far away. We'll have to get going."

"I will have your horses prepared," Father Chavez said and left the room.

Carolyn and Father Sacramente were awake now.

Lopez looked out the small window. "How long can we last outside on a night like this?" he muttered bitterly, mostly to himself.

Taylor turned to Father Sacramente and Carolyn and said, almost apologetically, "If we stay here, King will catch us. There just isn't anything we can do."

Father Sacramente smiled at him. It was a tired smile. "It's all right, Ford. It isn't your fault," he tried to assure him.

Father Chavez came in the door with sheepskins in his arms. "I have brought a sheepskin coat for each of you. They're very warm."

As they put the coats on, Lopez said quietly to the monk, "Do you know of any place we can go? We're not going to last long out there."

"I can give you some guidance," the monk said. "I'll show you."

Xoactl was still asleep. Carolyn wrapped a sheepskin coat around him and picked him up. Then Father Chavez led the way down the long corridor to the rear of the building.

The young monk brought the horses out of the stable and helped Father Sacramente and Carolyn mount up. They moved across to the gate, and Father Chavez walked with them and pointed down the valley.

"Down this way about five miles you will come to a sheepherder's cabin. You can take shelter there. From there on the trail goes downhill to the valley and is easy. Then about another seven miles from the cabin you will come to the border post of the United States Army from Fort Huachuca."

They moved out, with the two men leading the horses as before, Carolyn and Xoactl on one and Father Sacramente on the other.

"Thanks for your help," Taylor said to the old monk as they left.

"Vaya con Dios, my son," Father Chavez called. "Go with God."

The night was dark and cold, and it had begun snowing lightly again. Taylor put one foot in front of the other and doggedly moved ahead. He was aware only of the ground in front of him, the horse that he was leading, and the wind and the cold.

He had no idea how long they had gone when he was suddenly brought to reality by the neighing of a horse in front of him.

Father Sacramente had fallen from the saddle and was lying on the ground. Lopez had let go of the horse to help the old priest, and suddenly the horse bolted and ran, the sound of its galloping hooves growing fainter in the distance.

Lopez had the priest up on his feet and held him by sheer strength. Taylor hesitated.

"Go on! Go on," Lopez urged. "I saw the cabin. Get Carolyn and the boy to it. Then come back and help us."

Taylor moved ahead, holding the horse's bridle. Now he saw the sheepherder's cabin loom in the blackness. He helped Carolyn and Xoactl down off the horse and got the door of the cabin open. It was musty inside, but it was warm.

He struck a match and lit the coal-oil lantern they found on the small table. Then he handed Carolyn a couple more matches to start the fire going. She lay the boy down, and Taylor went back outside.

The other horse was gone. Taylor

looked quickly around, but he could not see the animal. He moved up the trail until he found Lopez and Father Sacramente.

"Leave me. Just leave me," the old priest gasped.

The two men ignored the statement, and together they supported the older man and all but carried him down the trail. Carolyn had left the door open a little so that the last way down the trail was lit by light from the lantern and the fire she had started inside.

Taylor and Lopez, on the verge of exhaustion, staggered through the door and lay the old priest down before they, too, collapsed onto the floor.

Chapter Fourteen

Ford Taylor came awake suddenly, and it took him a few minutes to realize where he was. The fire still burned in the small fireplace in the corner. That, and the crack around the door, gave enough light to see inside the cabin.

He sat up slowly, and as he did so, Lopez, who had been sleeping next to him, woke up. "How are you doing?" Lopez asked.

"I feel terrible," Taylor answered.

"You didn't move after you fell on the floor last night," Lopez said. "You were pretty well exhausted."

Taylor looked over to where Carolyn, Father Sacramente, and Xoactl slept on the other side of the cabin floor.

"How is he?" Taylor asked quietly.

"He had had a heart seizure when we got him into the cabin last night. Carolyn got more of the nitroglycerine into him, and that seemed to keep him alive."

171

"He's in pretty bad shape then?" Taylor asked.

"He couldn't go another step on his own. And, in case you don't remember, both horses ran off last night." Lopez got to his feet. "Since it's morning, I'll go outside and get some idea of where we are."

As the door closed behind Lopez, Carolyn stirred and then she sat up. "Ford, are you all right?" she asked.

"Yes. I think I'll live. Jose has gone out to look around."

She got up and put a couple of pieces of wood on the fire, then came over to sit beside him.

He took hold of her hand. "You look pretty worn out yourself," he told her. "Father Sacramente?" It was a question.

"Not very good. We need to get him to a doctor and a hospital."

"How's Xoactl?"

She smiled. "This seems to be just what he's needed. He seems to be stronger than all the rest of us put together."

The door opened and closed with a blast of cold air, and Lopez came in and sat on the floor beside them.

"What's it like?" Taylor asked.

"Cold, but it's not snowing anymore,"

Lopez said. "It's all downhill from here to the border. Father Chavez told us that it's about seven miles from here." Then he looked over at the sleeping priest to make sure that he couldn't hear. "Father Sacramente will never make it," he went on.

"We could carry him," Taylor said.

Lopez shook his head. "We'd have enough trouble getting ourselves down there on foot. Even Carolyn would find it a struggle."

"Then what are we going to do?" Taylor asked. "We can't leave him."

There was a soft laugh from the other side of the cabin, and Father Sacramente said faintly, "You really don't have any choice, do you?"

"I won't do it!" Taylor exclaimed. "We can assume that King and his men spent the night at the mission and that they'll start out first thing this morning. He's come this far—you can bet that he won't stop."

"So what are we going to do?" Lopez asked. "Stay here and fight him off with a couple of rifles?"

"What are the alternatives? What do you suggest?" Taylor asked.

"If we got to the border fast enough,

you could get help from the United
States Army," Lopez said.

"And come right back here," Taylor
went on.

"Yes. They're bound to have some force
at the border in light of all the revolutionary activity that's going on here in
Mexico this close to them," Lopez said.

Taylor stood there, indecision clearly
on his face.

Carolyn then spoke up. "He's right,
Ford. It's the only thing to do. I'll stay
here with Father Sacramente."

"Now wait a minute!" Taylor started.

"I have to stay, Ford. Father Sacramente needs me. But you must take
Xoactl with you."

"But why, if we're coming back for all
of you?" Taylor said.

"You may not be in time," she said
simply.

She stood there in front of him and
smiled, and he could see the love in her
eyes. "Hurry back, Ford," she said.

"We're wasting time," Lopez said
tersely.

He took Taylor by the arm, and they
went to the door. Lopez turned and offered Carolyn his rifle.

She shook her head. "I couldn't use it,
Jose."

Lopez stepped over and picked up Xoactl from the floor.

"We'll be waiting for you, major," Father Sacramente said with a wan smile.

The two men went out the door, and Carolyn closed it behind them. Taylor felt a sinking feeling within him as the door closed. It seemed so final.

They started on the trail that led down the side of the mountain. Taylor soon realized how weak and tired he was, but he guessed that Lopez must be as tired as he, even though he was younger. When they stopped to rest Taylor offered to carry Xoactl.

Lopez handed him over, and they started walking again. Taylor felt his legs go suddenly rubbery, and he sank down to the ground, making sure that the boy did not hit the dirt.

Lopez took Xoactl back, and Taylor murmured an apology and struggled to his feet. Together they kept moving, over the rough terrain, down the trail that led to freedom. Taylor couldn't move as fast as Lopez, and he lagged behind. Lopez walked to the top of a rise and then called back. Taylor struggled up to the rise, and they looked down on the hut and the tents that marked the United

States border and the outpost of the United States Army.

The old cast-iron stove made the hut warm, and Lopez and Taylor sat close to the stove and sipped cups of coffee. The sergeant came back into the room.

"I've taken the boy to get some food," he said. "We'll have our medic check him over. But he seems to have survived the last few days better than the two of you."

"How much longer will your commanding officer be?" Taylor asked.

"Not long. It's a couple of miles back to Fort Huachuca, and it's just the time it takes for the horses to get there and back."

They heard the sound of horses' hooves outside.

"In fact," the sergeant said, "I'm sure that's him now."

Major Hatch was a tall, straight, military-looking individual. He pulled off his gloves and extended his hand.

"Colonel Taylor, sir, it's a pleasure to meet you."

"It's a pleasure to be here, major," Taylor assured him. "Did your lieutenant give you the whole story?"

"Yes. I think I've been briefed pretty well. Where is Don Garcia's son?"

"We are taking care of him in the mess tent right now, sir," the sergeant answered.

"What about Miss Smith and Father Sacramente, major?" Taylor said. "When can we start? I wanted to get right back there, but the lieutenant said he needed your approval."

"There's a little more to it than that," Major Hatch said. "General Pattison has the cavalry here at Fort Huachuca on alert. We are supposed to stop any incursion from Mexico into the United States. But, on the same note, I cannot send United States Army troops into Mexico. That could start a war."

"But that cabin is only six or seven miles from here," Taylor insisted. "We'd be over there and back before anyone knew."

"General Pattison and his staff are meeting right now," the major said. "I'll have to wait orders before I move. I'm sorry, Colonel Taylor." He turned to the sergeant. "I'd like to see the Garcia boy."

"Yes, sir."

The two of them left the hut. Taylor walked to the window and looked out. There were three horses tethered outside the border hut. He looked at the horses for a minute and then made his decision.

The corporal of the guard sat by the stove. Taylor whispered to Lopez, "Delay them for a few minutes. Let me get a head start."

He quickly slipped his coat on, picked up his rifle, and was out the door before the corporal realized what was happening. When the corporal started after Taylor, Lopez stood firmly in the doorway, smiling.

Almost casually, Taylor unhitched the horses from the rail, swung into the saddle of one and, leading the other two by the reins, rode away. He passed the guards standing on the roadway, and suddenly Major Hatch ran from the mess tent.

"You can't do this, sir!" he yelled at Taylor.

"You'll have to shoot me to stop me!" Taylor yelled back.

He knew that he couldn't push the horses to a gallop, but he did move them as fast as they could go up the trail. Less than an hour after leaving the border, he came up to the final slope that approached the sheepherder's hut.

From the rise above, hidden behind some scrub oak, the Mexican rebel army sergeant watched Taylor coming. As

Taylor got closer, the sergeant turned and hurried down to where Colonel King stood beside the cabin.

"One man is coming with three horses," the sergeant said.

King went up the trail to where he could see the man coming. King was bitter. He had lost all his men but the one sergeant. He had failed to stop Taylor and Lopez from taking Don Garcia's son out of the country, and he knew he would have to answer for that. But if he could take this American Army Intelligence officer back, things might go better for him with his own revolutionary army.

He ran back down the trail and went inside the cabin where the sergeant was guarding Carolyn Smith and Father Sacramente.

"It's Taylor!" King said. "I'll stay down here," he told the sergeant. "You go up by the trail. Let him get past you, and then we'll take him."

"Do you want him alive?" the sergeant asked.

"Absolutely!" King said.

The sergeant went out, closing the door behind him. King drew his six-gun. He smiled at Carolyn and the old priest.

"Don't either of you make a sound," he told them.

Taylor came up over the hill and looked down. There was nothing to indicate that anything had happened down at the hut. He pulled the rifle up and rested it across the saddle in front of him.

He urged the horses forward and was halfway down the slope when the cabin door banged open and Carolyn ran out. "Ford!" she screamed. "Look out behind you!"

Taylor let go of the reins of the other two horses and pulled back on the reins of his own horse, jerking it around as the sergeant appeared on the hill above him.

As the horse reared back, Taylor toppled out of the saddle and onto the ground. He rolled over and came up with the rifle still in his hands. As the horses moved around him, he waited for a clear view of the rebel sergeant. Then he fired twice with the rifle. The soldier crumpled and rolled down the hill.

Taylor turned and saw Carolyn in front of the cabin. King had hold of her with one hand, and his other hand held his six-gun pressed against her back.

"Let her go, King. Let both of them go. Take me," Taylor said.

"No bargains," King answered. "Throw your gun down."

Taylor threw the rifle away from him. King let go of Carolyn, and she ran to Taylor.

"How is Father Sacramente?" he asked.

"He's all right," she said. "What about Jose and Xoactl?"

"We got across the border, but the United States Army refused to cross back. I had to come alone."

"How lucky for me," King said with a smile. "You have caused me a great deal of trouble, Ford. I have chased you across northern Mexico, but finally I have caught you."

"Father Sacramente and Carolyn can't help you, King. Let them go. I won't cause you any trouble."

"They want to see you back at revolutionary army headquarters, Ford. They know about your intelligence work. When you go before the highest military court of the revolution, I want these two to be with you."

Taylor tensed himself. He decided that he had to try something even if he got killed in the attempt. His nerves were all taut.

Suddenly a voice called from the side, "King, Over here!"

King turned and went into a crouch,

thumbing the hammer of his six-gun back. Major Jose Lopez fired his repeating rifle three times in rapid succession, sketching a small triangle on King's chest. King slumped to the ground, frantically trying to bring up the six-gun, but he died as the revolver fell from his hand.

Major Hatch rode over the skyline on his horse and followed Lopez down to the cabin.

"What happened?" Taylor asked in relief. "I thought that the U.S. Army was supposed to stay on its side of the border."

"It still is," Lopez said. "But Major Hatch is a man of spirit. He decided that we could not let you come alone."

"What about General Pattison?" Taylor asked Hatch.

Major Hatch smiled. "I suspect that the general and his staff will still be meeting by the time we cross back into the United States. That's how generals and their staffs operate. They'll never know."

Taylor chuckled.

"How is Father Sacramente?" Lopez asked.

"He's pretty good for an old man," the priest said, standing in the doorway of the hut. "Nothing wrong with me that a good night's sleep and a decent meal won't cure."

"Then we'll have to get you to where we can get both of those immediately," Lopez said. He smiled. "Poor Major Hatch will be uncomfortable until we get back across the border."

They rounded up the horses and helped Carolyn and Father Sacramente mount up. The two of them, with Major Hatch and Major Lopez, started off up the slope toward the trail that led to the border.

Taylor sat in the saddle for a minute and looked down at the body of King, the man who had once been his friend, and felt a sadness.

But what mattered now was the future. His life was at a new starting point, and, as he rode up the trail toward where Carolyn waited, he was smiling.